Katie's Secret Admirer

www.holly-webb.com

Triplets

Katie's Secret Admirer

HOLLY WEBB

SCHOLASTIC

Scholastic Children's Books
An imprint of Scholastic Ltd
Euston House, 24 Eversholt Street
London, NW1 1DB, UK
Registered office: Westfield Road, Southam, Warwickshire, CV47 0RA
SCHOLASTIC and associated logos are trademarks and/or registered trademarks of
Scholastic Inc.

First published in the UK by Scholastic Ltd, 2005
This edition published by Scholastic Ltd, 2014

Text copyright © Holly Webb, 2005

The right of Holly Webb to be identified as the author
of this work has been asserted by her.

ISBN 978 1407 14479 5

British Library Cataloguing-in-Publication Data.
A CIP catalogue record for this book is available from the British Library.

Printed and bound by CPI Group (UK) Ltd, Croydon, CR0 4YY
Papers used by Scholastic Children's Books are made from wood grown in
sustainable forests.

1 3 5 7 9 10 8 6 4 2

This is a work of fiction. Names, characters, places, incidents and dialogues are products
of the author's imagination or are used fictitiously. Any resemblance to actual people,
living or dead, events or locales is entirely coincidental.

www.scholastic.co.uk

Chapter One

"Look! That's him!" Megan was so excited that her upside-down face nearly matched her red hair.

Katie peered round her own muddy knees and nodded. "Definitely! Oh, this is so cool!"

Practically all the girls' squad had now spotted the little party trooping across the field, and given up on warm-up exercises. There had been a bit of grumbling when Mrs Ross suggested Saturday morning training sessions to get them into really good shape for the next round of schools league matches, but the whole squad had made it to the playing fields on time today. The boys' team were there too, on the adjacent pitch – after the girls had beaten them hollow in the fund-raising match last term, Mr Anderson hadn't had much trouble convincing them that a spot of extra practice on Saturdays would be a good idea. Now everyone in both squads was muttering and pointing excitedly. The tall, good-looking man with Mrs Ross and Mr Anderson was Garth Owen, the footballer. He'd actually gone to Manor Hill School, years ago, and then he'd been on the youth team at Stallford, the local football club. Now he played for Spurs, but he came back home to Darefield quite often to see his family.

Today the Spurs striker was running a masterclass in ball skills for his old school, and everyone was desperate to play their best in front of such a star. Lots of parents had come to watch, too – altogether the atmosphere was fantastic. The local paper had even sent a reporter and photographer along to capture the event.

Mr Anderson and Mrs Ross gathered the

two junior squads together (the senior teams trained later in the evening instead of at weekends, as so many of them had Saturday jobs), and everybody looked hopefully at Garth Owen. What would he be like? When they'd found out that he was coming, a couple of weeks ago, Katie and Megan had looked him up online to find out more about his playing style. He wasn't one of those really aggressive forward players who just powered through the field; instead he was very fast and he had fantastic ball control – he ran rings round the opposing players. Katie reckoned this was good news for the girls' team – speed and ball control were their strong points too, and they might be able to pick up some really good tips. They watched eagerly as he took off his tracksuit – what did Premiership footballers wear to train in? It turned out to be a slightly scruffy T-shirt and shorts, and Katie nodded approvingly. She wasn't really into the whole football and fashion thing – she reckoned

3

David Beckham would have been a better football player if he hadn't spent so much time worrying about his hair. Garth Owen looked a bit like he hadn't even brushed his that morning.

He smiled around at them all. "OK, morning everybody."

"Morning," they chorused back shyly. Even the Year Eights were a bit overawed, Katie noticed – super-confident people like Sarah, the girls' team captain, and Josh Matthews, Year Eight stud (and her sister Annabel's current all-time best-ever pin-up boy since she'd starred in the school Christmas play with him last term).

"I need to do some warm-up exercises before we get on to the fun stuff – sorry about that, I know you've already done yours. Won't do any harm though. Ready?"

Everyone nodded eagerly. This was really exciting – even boring warm-up exercises were better with a professional footballer leading them. Ten minutes of bends and stretches later, and they were being organized into small groups to work on their ball control: tapping the ball from foot to foot on the ground, then in the air, which was tricky. The groups were mixed from the two squads, which was weird – there had been such bad feeling between the girls' and the boys' teams that practising together felt a bit uncomfortable. Still, a couple of the boys were mates from class, Katie told herself – it was really dumb that they had to be sworn enemies as soon as they got on to the pitch. Talking of sworn enemies, though – Katie decided to pretend that Max Cooper (deliberate leg-kicker, class idiot and general pain-in-the-bum) wasn't a few metres away. Actually, for once, Max seemed to be behaving himself – he was listening to Garth Owen as though the footballer was telling his group that week's winning lottery numbers.

Katie was carefully shifting her weight from side to side to balance the ball as Garth had suggested, when she noticed that he was watching their group. He nodded approvingly at her. "Very nice – good control there."

Everyone in the group looked envious as he went on to the next lot.

"Wow!" said Robin, a boy from Katie's class who'd just got into the boys' squad, although he hadn't actually played in any matches yet. He gazed wide-eyed at Katie. "That was so cool. Well done. I can't believe I'd just dropped the ball when he came to watch us."

Katie was pink with pleasure. "He's really nice – I hadn't expected him to be like that."

After a few more minutes of ball-skills, Garth yelled, "Right! How about some shooting practice?"

"Yeees!" Everyone cheered. However much the staff went on about defence and tactics, and team-play making everyone's place on the pitch important, there just was something really cool about having a shot at the goal.

"We need a goalie – any volunteers?" Katie

pushed Megan forward. "Go on! It'll be brilliant!" "I can't be in goal against Garth Owen! I'll mess it up, stop it!" Megan's heels were practically making furrows in the pitch as she tried to stop Katie from volunteering her. It was too late though – she'd been spotted. "Great – do you play in goal for the girls then?" Megan gazed back looking hunted, and stammered something unintelligible. Katie was about to stick up for her, when, surprisingly, the team captain Sarah did it instead. "Uh-huh, Megan's really good – she made some brilliant saves in the league final last term. We'd never have won without her."

Megan blushed happily. Sarah wasn't given to saying that kind of thing much, and the Year Sevens in the team sometimes felt the Year Eights were still rather high-and-mighty, so the praise came as a shock. She grabbed her goalkeeper's gloves, which she'd left on the side, and trotted over to the goal feeling a bit happier. It was still quite nerve-racking to turn round and see thirty people staring at her, though, and that wasn't even counting the mums and dads who'd come to watch the masterclass from the sidelines. She rubbed her gloved hands together nervously, and listened as Garth explained what he was going to get everybody to do – try to convince the goalie that the ball was going to one side of the net when really they were aiming for the other. He was going to demonstrate, with Megan as his hapless victim.

Katie watched interestedly. Megan was really good at this usually – it was almost as though she had some kind of mind-reading ability and could see through people trying to fake her. Not that she always caught the ball, of course, but she was almost always on the right side of the goal. Katie wondered if Garth was going to kick the ball at Megan as hard as he would in a normal match. The stats about him on the web had said that he could send a ball into the net at a hundred and thirty kilometres an hour. From the look on her face, Megan was remembering the same website. Luckily, he'd obviously decided that wasn't going to be necessary, and the ball he sent at Megan was just fast rather than looking like something shot out of a cannon. Megan didn't catch it, but neither was she deceived by his clever footwork – she had her fingertips to the ball, but the goal was so slippery after the disgusting January weather that her feet slid out from under her, and she ended up covered in mud.

There was a nasty snigger from somewhere behind Katie, and she wheeled round furiously. Of course – Max Cooper. He took every opportunity he could to get at the triplets and their mates.

"Like you could do any better, dogbreath!" Katie snarled. Then she turned back and yelled, "Yay, Megan! You were really close!" Lots of the girls started clapping, and Katie noticed Becky's boyfriend, David, joining in.

Not for the first time, she thought how *nice* David was. He was really good at football as well; he was super-fast.

Garth Owen was grinning at Megan too. "That was brilliant! You nearly had me there. Come on, let's have another go, and then we'll try and get someone else muddy." He lined up again, and Megan clapped her gloves together determinedly. This time. . .

Yes! There was an amazed gasp as Megan launched herself at the ball. There was no way she was missing this one, and besides, she already looked like a swamp monster so she didn't need to worry about a bit more mud. The ball didn't have a chance – thirty-eight kilos of determined Megan felled it to the ground with a thump.

Katie led a victory dance as the girls' squad went mad. Even Cara Peters, who she normally couldn't stand, was chanting "Go Meg-an! Go Meg-an!" with the others.

*

An hour later, everyone was milling around the school hall. The sports department had put out coffee and biscuits for everyone who'd been watching the session, so most of the squads' parents were chatting and watching as the players queued up for autographs. Lots of them had brought cameras and were snapping pictures of their sons and daughters with Garth Owen. Mrs Ryan waved across the room at Katie and Megan (now without her second skin of mud) as they stood in line, clutching pictures of him in Spurs kit that they'd downloaded from the net.

"I can't believe your photo's going to be in the paper!" said Katie for about the tenth time.

"I know! It's so cool – my dad reckons he's going to buy about five copies." Megan grinned all over her face. After her brilliant save, the newspaper photographer had insisted on taking several pictures of her and Garth, with Megan clutching the football and beaming like anything through a mask of mud.

"Don't get your hopes up, Megan. I bet you broke his camera, with a face like that."

Megan's face fell. However used they were to Max's evilness, he could still be shockingly horrible. Megan had been flying so high that Max's mean comment really hurt, and Katie could tell — her freckles were suddenly dark against her white face. Katie rounded on him furiously — how dare he spoil Megan's big moment?

"You really are a scumbag! Get lost — you're just jealous 'cause no one'll ever want to put a photo of something as disgusting as you in the paper."

Max sneered at her, but he obviously couldn't think of anything to say, and after a few prickly moments he gave them one last smirk and wandered off. Not far, though — he got about three steps and stopped dead. He'd obviously been going to find his dad, but then realized with horror that he was talking to Katie's mother.

"What does *she* want, talking to my dad?" he snarled back at Katie.

Katie's face was a mask of contempt as she replied, "How should I know? What does he want talking to her? Why don't you both just *get lost!*" She practically spat the last two words, and Max took a step back – she looked so angry.

He recovered quickly though: "I bet she's having a go at him about me – have you been whining to Mummy again?" Max had deliberately injured Katie's leg in a match the previous term, and Mrs Ryan had phoned up his dad to complain.

"As if! I don't need anybody's help to deal with you. I never wanted her to phone your dad in the first place." Katie folded her arms and glared and Max glared back. It was a stand-off, and it only ended because Katie and Megan had, without even noticing, got to the front of the autograph queue. Max was dismissed without another thought as they hurled eager questions at Garth Owen.

Once they'd got their photos signed, and had to reluctantly let the next people in the line have their turn, Katie and Megan wandered off in search of their parents.

"You know," said Megan thoughtfully, "I don't think your mum *was* having a go at Max's dad earlier."

"No?" Katie didn't sound that interested. She was sick to death of Max, and his dad.

"No. She looked as though they were just – chatting. She was smiling at him."

Katie looked sharply at her. "What do you mean?"

"They looked as though they were friends, I suppose."

"No way!" Katie laughed. "Sorry, Megan, but that's silly – this is the first time they've spoken to each other. Anyway how could my mum be friends with someone who has a son like *Max*?"

Megan just shrugged. Katie headed over to her mum, now chatting to Megan's parents.

She couldn't help looking at Mum carefully, even though she'd laughed off Megan's silly idea. *Had* she been making friends with Max's dad? *Why?* And why couldn't Katie get the horrible image of the two of them smiling at each other out of her head?

Chapter Two

Once she got home, Katie discovered that however much she'd laughed at Megan about her mum and Mr Cooper being friendly – or more than friendly – the thought just wouldn't go away. It *was* stupid – wasn't it? They'd just been talking, like parents did at these things. It didn't mean anything. Still, she found as she wandered up the stairs to change that she very much wanted to talk to Becky and Bel about this. She needed someone to tell her, very firmly, that of course it was totally mad, and preferably laugh themselves silly at the same time.

Unfortunately, she'd forgotten that both her sisters had their own plans that morning.

Becky was meeting up with David after the football session so they could go into town and look at Valentine's Day presents for each other. Katie was surprised at herself for forgetting – she and Bel had spent enough time teasing Becky about how she and David were so couply and sad that they were practically *married*. But Katie had a feeling that Bel wouldn't have minded someone to be like that with. She shuddered. Maybe when she was a bit older she'd want to go out with someone, but the idea of spending a perfectly good Saturday looking at pink teddy bears was truly awful.

Bel had gone to Saima's to try out some fantastic new make-up tricks that one of their magazines had come up with. Katie had a strong suspicion that she wouldn't be able to tell the difference when Bel came back flaunting her new look, but she supposed it would be cruel not to pretend a bit. She flung herself down on her bed crossly. Both her sisters seemed to be obsessed with *boys* at the moment. Becky never seemed to move without David following her like some kind of . . . some kind of . . . *puppy* (Katie had the grace to feel guilty for thinking this: David was really nice, even if she wished he wasn't around quite so much), and Bel was spending the whole time obsessing about how she looked, and whether she was pretty enough for Josh Matthews to notice or not. He'd been Prince Charming to her Cinderella in the school play, and he'd had to kiss her in front of about two hundred people. Unfortunately, he wasn't showing any signs of doing it again. And now that Valentine's Day was getting close, the whole thing seemed to have moved up a gear.

Katie rolled over and stared up at the ceiling, her arms behind her head. She felt wrong. It was Becky that normally worried herself silly about stuff like this, and Bel was the one who claimed to know everything there was to know about relationships, so why was it her, Katie, trying to work out what was going on between her mum and Max's dad? She stood up suddenly, and shook herself, her long ponytail swinging. There was no point bothering herself about it – because it was *not* happening. Megan was wrong, full stop. So what if they'd been chatting and smiling? Mum was nice, and polite, and she felt really sorry for Max and his dad, she'd said so. That was all.

By the time Bel and Becky got home Katie had calmed down a bit. Besides, she was so determined that Megan had to be wrong that she decided not to even mention it to her sisters.

As she'd thought, Bel didn't look all that different, just a bit surprised somehow. Katie looked at her sister curiously. "What have you done to your face? It looks – different. . ."

Annabel gave a long-suffering sigh. "I've got dots of white eyeliner at the corners of my eyes – look." She loomed over Katie, who was curled up on the sofa, and opened her eyes scarily wide.

Katie recoiled. "Um, yes. Why? You just look kind of surprised."

Annabel's showing-off-eyeliner face mutated into a glare. "I do not! My eyes are like melting pools! The magazine said so!"

That brought Katie out of her edgy mood. She laughed.

"What?" Annabel asked indignantly. "What's so funny? Has it smudged?" She ran to the mirror to check.

"Melting pools!" Katie sniggered.

"Oh, shut up," her sister said disgustedly. "You don't understand anything."

"I do," said Katie. "I'm sure Josh will love it."

Over by the mirror, Annabel scowled at her perfectly made-up face. She really wasn't sure what was going on with Josh. He smiled and said hello when they met each other in the corridor, but he never made an effort to talk to her on purpose, and she was wondering whether to give up. She certainly wasn't going to throw herself at him – that would be way too embarrassing. Annabel was used to being the one that boys made fools of themselves over, and she found fancying somebody who didn't seem to fancy her back a bit weird.

Becky walked in just then and gave Annabel a horrified stare. "What have you done to your face?" she gasped in a really shocked voice.

"Thanks a bunch, Becky!" Annabel snarled, and she stormed out.

Becky turned to Katie with a "What did I say?" look on her face. Katie missed it entirely, though, because she was laughing so much she'd buried her face in the sofa cushions. When she eventually recovered, she beamed at her sister and asked, "So did you have a good time? What are you going to get him?"

"Mmmm, it was fun. First we had hot chocolate in one of those posh coffee shops, and then we went in that new bath stuff shop,

Bliss, you know, by the cinema? The only thing is once you've been in there five minutes you can't smell anything. It's like your nose goes on strike. I think David might get me some stuff from there."

"Bel'll be jealous."

Becky grinned. "I know. I still can't decide whether to get David some chocolate or this really cute pink dinosaur I found. I mean, chocolate doesn't last, but do boys actually *like* furry things? I'm just not sure."

"Haven't a clue," said Katie cheerfully. "To be perfectly honest, I reckon even if you bought David a pink furry dinosaur and told him he had to eat it, he'd still do it, so he's going to like anything you buy him. He's the soppiest person I've ever met apart from you. But a good footballer," she admitted, consideringly.

Becky actually looked pleased at this, which just proved how soppy she was, Katie thought. Watching her little sister (well, only by about ten minutes, but Katie reckoned it still counted) smile secretly to herself, and wind her hair round her fingers in a smugly contented fashion, Katie did wonder if she was missing something. But she just couldn't imagine spending a morning gazing into someone's eyes over hot chocolate, even if there *was* whipped cream and even if they were the best footballer in the world.

On Monday morning, Annabel's miffed mood had gone completely, although Katie noticed that she hadn't reapplied the white eyeliner. She also seemed to have come to a decision about Josh.

"Forget him," she said firmly, waving her toast and Marmite at Katie. "Not worth worrying about. He's far too obsessed with his looks anyway."

"Oh, *you* can talk," Katie muttered into her cereal, but she was smiling inside. Josh Matthews was a snake, as far as she was concerned, and she and Becky and all their mates had been really worried about Annabel's thing for him.

"No, he's far too immature," Annabel carried on, in the tone of someone desperately trying to convince herself as well as everyone else. "And too keen on football. Sorry, Becky, I know David likes it too, but I get quite enough football stuff at home from Katie."

Becky and Katie just grinned at each other in relief as Annabel applied herself to her toast. Mum looked fairly pleased too, Katie noticed – she was very good at not telling the triplets who they ought to be friends with, she liked them to work those sort of things out for themselves, but she'd picked up on Katie and Becky's not-so-subtle hints that Josh was bad news.

Monday morning dragged, as always. Whoever had worked out the timetable seemed to have planned it deliberately – coming up with the worst possible combination for Year Sevens who still wanted it to be the weekend.

Monday mornings ought to ease them in gently, Katie thought. Double maths with a grumpy Mr Jones who looked like he was wishing it was still the weekend too was not ideal. He kept turning round to the whiteboard so he could yawn, and the rest of the class were practically asleep in their textbooks. Katie actually liked maths, and was very good at it, but trigonometry wasn't fun first thing on a Monday morning.

The triplets turned up in the dining hall feeling like they really deserved lunch. They settled at one of the long tables with Megan, Saima, Becky's best mate Fran, and David. He'd got a bit of stick from some of the boys in their class about sitting with a bunch of girls, but he was one of those people who didn't much mind what everyone else thought. Katie was hoping that would rub off on Becky, who tended to dissolve into tears if anyone so much as gave her a nasty look. Anyway, David had obviously converted some of them, because

Robin and his mate Jack wandered over with their trays, looking slightly sheepish.

"Hi," said Robin, who seemed to be leading the pair of them – in fact, was Katie imagining it, or did Jack look as though he hadn't exactly been expecting to end up at a table full of girls? "Um, is anyone sitting here?" He waved his tray at the empty seats and Fran had to field his apple pie and custard as it slithered dangerously close to her lap.

"Sorry!" Robin gabbled, an embarrassed expression on his face.

Katie grinned at him. "I'd sit down before you lose that for good."

Robin blushed but looked pleased. He sat down quickly, and Jack followed, still looking a bit reluctant, Katie thought. Robin stared down at his plate, and started eating as though his life depended on it. Boys were so odd.

Jack had obviously decided to make the best of things, and started telling Becky about a snake he'd seen in the exotic pet shop in

Stallford. He was a huge reptile fan and already had a pet lizard.

"It's fantastic! Really huge – that's the problem, though, you see, I'd need a massive vivarium, practically the size of my bedroom. And my mum's not keen. I dragged her into the shop and showed her – I thought she'd love it, you know, as she quite likes Godzilla, but she nearly had a fit. She reckoned it could down my little sister in a couple of mouthfuls. Personally I don't think that's much of a problem," Jack added gloomily. "But Mum said over her dead body. It would have been birthdays and Christmases for about the next ten years as well: snakes are *really* expensive."

"Hi, you lot!"

Katie and the others looked up, surprised – what was this, rush hour?

Then her face fell. It was Josh Matthews. Just when Annabel had finally come to her senses! Katie stared worriedly at Annabel, who was consciously trying to seem unconcerned by the arrival of one of the most popular boys in Year Eight.

"Hey Annabel. How's it going?"

Annabel managed (by an enormous effort) to sound relaxed and confident as she smiled back and said, "Oh, fine."

OK, it wasn't the most exciting thing she could have said, but at least she'd managed to string coherent noises together when her brain had just gone into overdrive. *What was he doing here?* She felt like she needed to call time out for a strategy meeting with Saima or something.

Josh looked round at the rest of the table and smiled faintly, as though they were lower lifeforms and he was gracing them with his presence. Everyone stared back as though they weren't feeling particularly graced. Then he turned his charm on Annabel. "Do you mind coming over here a minute? I just wanted to talk to you – er – *privately*." He jerked his head meaningfully at the others.

Annabel blinked, and then got up very, very

carefully – it would be too embarrassing to knock her chair over or something like that, and she felt worryingly clumsy. She followed Josh over to one of the big pillars covered in posters advertising horrible school food, and he leaned up against it looking like something out of a fashion magazine, even in school uniform. So Annabel thought, anyway. To the others, who were watching and desperately trying to overhear, he looked a bit less glamorous.

David made a face. "He really loves himself," he said disgustedly. "Look at him, clocking whether everyone's watching him."

The others nodded, staring resignedly as Josh quite obviously asked Annabel out, and she, even more obviously, said yes.

Saima tutted. "'Honestly. She could be a bit more subtle about it. She practically hugged him on the spot."

Josh sauntered off, looking pleased with himself, and leaving Annabel to wander dazedly back – though not too dazedly to notice Amy Mannering's furious face as she passed her table. Annabel grinned – so Amy was jealous, was she? Things were just getting better and better! When she got back to her own table she was greeted with a barrage of glares, but she didn't seem to notice.

"He asked me out," she murmured blissfully. Katie and Becky just looked at each other and sighed.

Chapter Three

After they'd all finished lunch, Katie and Megan left the others gossiping and went off to see if Mrs Ross had put up the team list for that week's league fixture. By now they were both pretty much dead certs for the team – and as Katie said, "Mrs Ross wouldn't dare drop Garth Owen's favourite goalie" – but they always checked the board, just in case. Usually there would be a few other people checking the various fixture lists, but today there seemed to be loads. Katie and Megan exchanged puzzled looks and went closer. Everyone was staring at a huge pink poster that Mrs Armstrong, the deputy head, was pinning up.

Katie stood on tiptoe and peered at the

poster. "A *Valentine's Ball?*" She couldn't really have sounded less excited. In fact, she sounded as though she wanted to be sick.

Megan wrinkled her nose. "Is it just me, or is everyone obsessed with Valentine's Day right now?"

Katie nodded, then went on reading the poster and giggled. "Look when it is!"

"Friday – that must be next Friday? Oh, no!" Megan worked out why Katie was sniggering, and joined in. "Friday 13th? Whose idea was *that*?" she snorted.

"This must be another fund-raising thing for the swimming pool," Katie decided. "How much are the tickets?"

Megan peered over several people's shoulders. "Two pounds – I suppose it's not bad. I can think of much better things to do with a Friday night than stand around the school hall though."

Katie looked thoughtful. "You know, Megan, you've just given me a really good idea."

"What?"

"Better things to do! OK, so let's do them – let's have our own party."

"You think *we* should have a Valentine's party?"

"*No!* We're going to have an anti-Valentine's party. No boys, no pink. And no fluffy animals whatsoever," Katie added, thinking of Becky's dinosaur dilemma.

"Oh, what, watch action films, that kind of thing?" Megan was getting into the spirit of it now.

"Yeah, and – and eat curry!" Katie was trying to think as unromantically as possible.

"But I don't like curry – and you don't either," pointed out Megan reasonably.

"Noooo, I suppose not. But you know what I mean."

"Uh-huh – this is such a cool idea, Katie," Megan said seriously. "I'm getting *so* sick of Valentine's Day stuff everywhere."

"I know, it's like everyone's got pink fluff for

brains lately. Let's go and tell the others the plan!"

Thinking about it later that evening, Katie realized that she and Megan had been really stupid – they'd got carried away with their cool idea, and not actually thought it through. But at the time, as they raced back to their classroom, they were bubbling with enthusiasm. Becky, Fran, Bel and Saima were sitting on their desks talking excitedly about something when Katie and Megan skidded up to them.

"We've got brilliant news!" Katie panted.

The others looked a bit surprised. "About the party?" Bel asked, in a slightly confused voice – *Katie*, really excited about a Valentine's party?

"Yeah!" Katie nodded vigorously, then stopped. How did Bel know about their plan already? Unless. . .

"Doesn't it sound great?" Saima squealed. "Bel thinks Josh is going to ask her to go!"

Ah. Suddenly Katie realized that her sisters and their mates were getting all excited about the very party that she and Megan were trying to avoid.

"Oh. You don't *really* want to go to that thing, do you?" she asked, clinging to a last shred of hope. "It's going to be totally sad – we've got a much better idea."

"What?" Bel put in sceptically. She couldn't imagine an alternative that would be more fun than a dance where the whole school saw that she was going out with Josh Matthews.

Katie took a deep breath, and smiled determinedly. "Megan and I think we should have an anti–Valentine's party. You know, no boys, just all of us – kind of a – a girl power thing!" she finished triumphantly.

"No boys?" Becky echoed, worriedly. She was sure David would want to go to the school party with her.

"No, just us," Katie said impatiently. "What do we need the boys for?"

Annabel and Becky exchanged glances, and then stared at the floor. With Becky spending so much time with David, and Bel all caught up in the whole Josh thing, it was obvious that Katie would feel a bit left out, and they really didn't want to upset her – but they so wanted to go to the ball!

Katie looked quickly at her sisters' identical sheepish faces, and gathered that there was a crushing lack of enthusiasm for her big plan. She sighed crossly, and glared at Becky. "I suppose *David* is taking you to this thing then?" she snapped.

Becky gave a tiny shrug, still not looking at her sister. "Maybe," she said in a small voice. "He had to go and see Mr Anderson about something, so I haven't talked to him about it. Look, I'm sorry, Katie!" She finally glanced up. "I know you don't want to go, but it sounds really fun! There's going to be a DJ, and we can all dance together – it won't just be me and David and Bel and Josh, we'll all be in a gang.

Please say you'll come. You do *like* dancing. It won't be as much fun without you two there." Becky gazed beseechingly at Katie and Megan, and the others looked at them hopefully.

"I won't even make you dress up!" Bel added, which was the ultimate offer from someone so clothes-conscious.

Katie sighed. "So I could wear my football shirt?" she asked slyly.

Annabel's face contorted, as though in actual pain. "I suppose. If you *must*," she said through gritted teeth.

Katie glanced at Megan to see what she thought. She looked disappointed, and Katie could understand why – their party plan had seemed so much more fun!

"I know!" She grinned encouragingly at Megan. "Me and Megan will come to the school party on the Friday, but then you have to come to our party the next day! That's Valentine's Day anyway. It'll be much better to have the no-boys party then – more meaningful."

She nodded, pleased with the idea. "OK?" she asked hopefully, gazing round at the others.

Annabel was looking unsure. "But Josh might want me to do something with him that day!" she said worriedly. "I'm sure he will, I mean if we're going out together he's bound to want to see me on Valentine's Day." Her eyes glazed over slightly as she imagined Josh taking her out somewhere really romantic.

Surprisingly, it was Saima who disagreed with her. "You know, Bel, I think you've got to be careful. You haven't even been on one date yet. You don't want to come across too keen. If he does ask you out on the Saturday evening, just tell him you've got plans with your friends. You don't want him thinking he can just snap his fingers and you'll come running."

Even though Katie thought this sounded very like the ditzy relationship advice from the letters page of Annabel and Saima's favourite magazine, she wasn't going to argue. "Exactly. It's about time somebody stood up to Josh Matthews a bit." She leaned closer to Annabel, with a very serious expression on her face. "You know what Julianne was like – she ran after him like a little lapdog. You don't want him thinking he can order *you* about like that, do you?"

Julianne had been Josh's previous girlfriend, and he'd been really mean to her. It was one of the reasons why Katie and Becky had been hoping the whole Josh thing would come to nothing. They really didn't want Annabel going out with a slimeball. But at least they could try to make sure she wasn't at his beck and call all the time. Only Katie was allowed to boss her sisters around!

Annabel looked thoughtful. She had no idea why Katie and Becky had taken against Josh – but maybe the others were right. Playing a bit hard to get was important; after all, she didn't want to look desperate! "I suppose we could do something in the daytime instead," she mused.

"Exactly!" Katie cheered. "We're on then. Me and Megan will start planning what we're going to do."

Chapter Four

The triplets raced home from school to tell their mum about the plans: Katie had realized halfway through French that she'd arranged a sleepover party and told everybody it was happening without asking Mum first. But she was fairly sure Mum wouldn't mind.

Annabel was first in with the news though, dashing through the front door as soon as Katie had unlocked it, slinging her coat and bag vaguely in the direction of the banisters and racing for the kitchen. Mrs Ryan liked working at the kitchen table – it meant easy access to coffee, and the biscuit tin, and being able to keep an eye on whatever was for tea.

"Mum, Mum! Guess what!" Annabel

skidded into the kitchen, hair streaming behind her.

Mrs Ryan made a split-second grab for the papers she was working on to stop Annabel from sending them flying.

"Er—" Mrs Ryan was thinking, but Annabel was too excited to wait for her.

"Josh asked me out!"

"Oh!" The triplets' mum had heard quite a lot about Josh Matthews. She'd never actually met him, but she'd seen him in the play with Annabel, and she was inclined to believe Katie and Becky – he had *looked* a bit too good to be true. "Oh, that's nice, darling," she managed.

"Nice?" Annabel looked suspiciously at her mother. "Oh, don't say you don't like him either? You've never even met him, it's not fair!"

"Bel! I only said it was nice – really, darling, I'm pleased for you."

Annabel humphed. Nobody had reacted properly to her news. Even Saima had warned her to be careful. It would have been really good if just one person had jumped up and down and hugged her and told her that it was fab.

Mrs Ryan was now listening to Becky, who had started telling her about the Valentine's Ball at school.

David had rather shyly come up to her at the end of school and asked if she wanted to go.

"It was really sweet, Mum, he looked as though he thought I might say no – he went all shy. But the party's going to be brilliant, it's a proper dance, with a DJ and everything. We can go, can't we?"

Listening to her, Katie suddenly felt like Becky had disappeared and she had two Annabels instead. It was very weird. Sweet, quiet, animal-loving Becky seemed to have been replaced by a changeling sister who wanted to talk about boys and discos. It helped a bit that Pixie, their little black cat, came in just then and weaved her way round Becky's ankles, purring lovingly (she wouldn't do that to anyone else in the family: they were more likely to get their toes bitten off). Katie huffed out through her nose – Valentine's Day! There were nearly two weeks to go and she was sick to death of it already.

Mum was disappointingly enthusiastic about the Valentine's Ball, wanting Becky and Bel to tell her all the details. Katie listened irritably, waiting for a chance to break in and ask about her sleepover party.

"Apparently they're going to decorate the hall and everything, with loads of pink balloons—"

"And silver streamer things," Annabel put in.

"Yes, and there's a dress code, so you can't wear your ratty trainers Katie!"

"No trainers?" Katie's voice dripped with disgust. "Oh, great, so now I have to wear my school shoes with my football shirt?"

Mum looked confused. "I don't think you

can wear a football shirt, darling, not if it's supposed to be smart."

"Annabel said I could," Katie snapped back grumpily. She was amazed to see Becky and Annabel exchange smiling but slightly long-suffering glances over her head (or so they thought). What did they think they were doing? *She* did that – with Becky to express secret amusement at Annabel's weirder ways, or with Annabel when Becky was being particularly mouse-ish.

Annabel looked at her smugly. "That was before we agreed to your party idea. If we're giving up our Valentine's evening to come to that, then you can at least dress nicely the day before. Mum, Katie wants to have a sleepover on Valentine's Day. Can we?"

Annabel sounded slightly bored and contemptuous of the idea – as though a sleepover was somehow babyish compared to the real party on the Friday! When Katie and Megan had thought of it, the whole idea had seemed so grown-up and sophisticated, and now Annabel was making her sound like a sulky little girl as she prattled on to Mum. "Katie doesn't really want to come on Friday, so we're having the sleepover for her. No boys allowed." Annabel giggled.

"It's not like that," Katie burst out crossly. Even Mum's understanding smile was rubbing her up the wrong way now. "Me and Megan were just getting sick of the way everyone's obsessed with Valentine's Day, that's all. We thought it would be cool to do something totally different. You don't *have* to come!"

"We want to," Becky assured her. "It sounds good. Sleepovers are always fun. Please can we, Mum?"

"Just you three and Megan, Saima and Fran?" Mum asked. The triplets nodded eagerly. "Fine by me, as long as you clear up." Mum sounded quite happy with the plan, but Katie was left feeling as though her party had been hijacked – it wasn't just a sleepover, it was a protest, and nobody was taking it seriously enough.

As the triplets walked to school on Tuesday morning, Katie's cross mood seemed to have settled in to stay. The weather didn't help. A horrible cold drizzle was falling, and it felt as if it was seeping right through to her bones. Katie shook off the little lake that had dribbled down inside her hood, and kicked irritably at a puddle.

"Hey!" Annabel snapped. "You're splashing me, stop it!"

Katie stalked on ahead – her feet were soaked now, too, and she just wanted to get inside.

Finally they reached the school, and flung themselves into their classroom. There was a smell of wet day hanging about – soaked coats were steaming on the radiators, umbrellas were dripping all over the floor, and groups of

47

damp people were huddled up on the desks shivering together.

Megan and Fran were sitting together, looking worriedly at Fran's homework diary, which had been in a not-quite-closed pocket on the front of her rucksack. Fran carefully turned the limp pages, and sighed.

"It might be OK if you put it on the radiator," Megan suggested. "Oh, hi, you three! Isn't it horrible out there?"

"We're soaked," Katie agreed, dumping her bag on one of the chairs and feeling better at the sight of Megan's cheerful face and bouncy red curls – which were even bouncier than usual, as the wet weather seemed to have sent them a bit mad.

"Becky, look!" moaned Fran worriedly. "Do you think Miss Fraser will let me have a new one?" She waved the soggy book at her friend, and the cover started to detach itself from the pages.

"Nope," said Jack. He picked up the sad wet

thing between finger and thumb and grinned. "You'll have to wring it out and dry it with a hairdryer." He winked at Robin who was watching from his desk.

Becky was a bit more sympathetic. "Ignore him, Fran! I think Megan's right, it'll be fine if you leave it on the radiator for a while."

"You should put it under a pile of books," Robin said, sounding rather nervous as he came closer and stood next to Katie.

Everyone stared at him – what on earth was he talking about?

Robin went a bit pink, and explained, "To stop it going all crinkly when it dries. My mum did that with a library book that my sister dropped in the bath."

"Did it work?" asked Fran anxiously.

"Mostly. It took ages though – but that was a whole book."

"There you go then – put it in your locker with loads of stuff on top." Katie grinned at Robin, which made him even pinker – problem solved. "Did anybody see the football on TV last night?" She and Robin plunged into a discussion of the match and Jack joined in — he loved talking football even though he wasn't a brilliant player himself.

They kept chatting until registration, listening to the rain making huge puddles in the playground. The others chipped in occasionally, but mostly talked about the Valentine's Ball – *again*.

"Are you going to that thing?" Katie asked the boys, in disgust.

Jack shrugged. "Maybe. Oh, I'm not *asking* anybody to it, but I might just go – could be fun. What d'you reckon, Robin?"

"Um, yeah. Are you going, Katie?"

"They're making me. I think it's going to be awful though."

"Cool." Robin seemed to realize that this was a slightly weird answer to what Katie had just said, because he went pink again and stared at his feet.

50

Jack and Katie both gave him a bit of a funny look, but then Annabel broke in to ask Jack's view on Saima's new nail polish – she said they wanted a boy's opinion. Jack stammered out something along the lines of not knowing anything about nail polish and caring less, but he wasn't very convincing, especially when Saima fluttered her eyelashes at him, and all the girls, even Katie, giggled. That was when Jack and Robin decided it was definitely time to get back to their own table, as Miss Fraser was just coming in to do the register.

"I know it's in here somewhere!" It was later that morning and Katie was frantically rummaging through her rucksack, searching for her French exercise book. Mr Hatton, their fearsome French teacher, was due any minute, and his was not the kind of lesson you forgot a book for.

"You didn't leave it in your locker?" Megan

asked, leaning over to look in the rucksack as well.

"Don't think so – no, I had it last night to look at that vocab we had to learn. Oh, *please* don't let me have left it at home!" Katie had thrown practically the whole contents of her rucksack over the table by now, and was digging frantically at the bottom.

"Here it is! Oh, wow, I was really panicking." She whisked the book out, bringing a piece of folded paper with it, then quickly stuffed everything else back in so as to have the table tidy before Mr Hatton arrived.

"What's that?" Megan asked, tweaking the paper that was sticking out of the book – she could see some writing that didn't look like Katie's.

"No idea." Katie pulled it out, unfolded it, and read it. Then she read it again, confused.

YOU'RE BRILLIANT AT FOOTBALL.
I REALLY LIKE YOU!

She crumpled it up quickly, feeling totally embarrassed.

"What is it?" asked Megan again, interestedly.

"Nothing. Just something of Bel's."

Megan nodded and turned the conversation to the impossibility of their French homework, and Katie managed to make some vaguely sensible answers. What on earth was going on? Was it some kind of joke? If it hadn't been for the football thing she'd have supposed the note was meant for Annabel, but no one would write *that* to her.

It was lucky that Mr Hatton was in a particularly good mood (for him, anyway) or he might have noticed that Katie really wasn't concentrating on the class's visit to the *boulangerie*. She really couldn't have cared less how many croissants they were buying, all she could think about was that stupid note.

"Are you OK?" whispered Megan, taking

her life into her hands as Mr Hatton turned to write something on the board. "I think you just wrote down that the baker sold you an elephant."

Katie jumped, and realized that she'd better concentrate or she'd be in trouble. "Tell you at break," she hissed. She really needed to talk about this to somebody, and preferably not someone who was obsessed with romance, which obviously cut out her sisters.

It was still pouring down at breaktime, which made it a bit difficult for Katie and Megan to find anywhere private to talk. After discounting what seemed like most of the school because somebody else was already occupying it, they finally found an empty table in the library. They could talk here as long as they didn't make enough noise to attract the attention of the librarian.

"So what's up?" murmured Megan. "Are you upset because of Becky and Bel being so stupid about boys and Valentine's Day?" She tended to get right to the point.

"No. Well, yes, that too. But – oh, just look at this!"

Katie handed over the scrunched-up note, and sat back, watching Megan and worrying about what her plain-speaking mate would say. Suddenly she wished she had told Bel and Becky – at least she had a good idea how they'd react.

Megan looked up, her eyes round with surprise. "Wow," she said thoughtfully. "Have you got any idea who it's from?"

Katie shook her head, relieved – Megan hadn't laughed at her, which was what she'd been dreading. "I haven't a clue. I mean, who on earth would send it? To me?"

Megan gazed down at the note doubtfully. "No idea." She held the paper out, frowning. "Suppose you don't recognize the handwriting?"

"Nope." Katie shook her head miserably.

"And it just turned up in my rucksack – you saw me find it, in French this morning."

"But who could've slipped it into your bag without you noticing?"

"I don't know!" Katie almost wailed – but then she remembered where they were so it came out as a strangled whisper.

Megan frowned down at the offending piece of paper. "I can't think of any way to find out who it's from. It's just going to have to be a mystery."

"I suppose," Katie muttered.

The thing was, the words *for now* seemed to be hanging in the air at the end of Megan's sentence.

Chapter Five

For the rest of the week, Katie guarded her rucksack like a starved Rottweiler, never letting it out of her sight, and practically baring her teeth at anyone who dared to brush past it. She got quite a few funny looks, but strangely, Becky and Annabel hardly seemed to notice. Annabel did ask her on Thursday why she was clutching her bag like it was going to run away, but that was about it. They were so taken up with the plans for the Valentine's Ball that they didn't have a lot of time for anything else, even strangely jumpy sisters.

Becky, Fran and David had helped to make scenery for the school play the previous term, and when the art teacher, Mrs Cranmer, found out that she'd been lumbered with decorating the school hall for the party, she'd remembered how useful they'd been. She collared them in art on Wednesday.

"We've got a budget of exactly nothing – you three were great with the scenery and I was wondering if you'd help out? In lunchtimes."

Becky nodded enthusiastically – painting the scenery had been loads of fun. She glanced hopefully at Fran and David, who were looking pleased. Suddenly Annabel nudged her, and mouthed, "Us too!" Saima was nodding urgently at Becky from her side of the table.

"That would be great, Mrs Cranmer. But do you think my sister could help too? And Saima? She and Fran can draw some hearts and arrows and things, can't you?"

"Cupids with bows, stuff like that?" asked Annabel hopefully. She loved doing this kind of thing and it sounded brilliant.

Mrs Cranmer looked delighted. "Excellent.

This is such a relief – normally I'd get the Year Elevens to help, but they're swamped with coursework. Thanks, all of you – see you in the art room at lunchtime!"

All of this meant that Katie, who was really *not* that artistic and hadn't wanted to join in, hardly saw her sisters, and when she did they were still so obsessed with pink and gold and heart-shaped cut-outs that she wished they'd stayed in the art room.

Katie wasn't sure whether or not to be grateful that there were no more notes – she really didn't want another one, of course, but she felt completely on edge. Every time she opened her rucksack she felt like she had to hunt carefully through all her stuff to make sure there wasn't another fateful note lurking somewhere inside. At least if there *was* it would put a stop to the suspense. She was worried that she was annoying Megan as well. Her friend was being really nice about the whole thing, but Katie felt like she hadn't done anything all week except tear the whole note thing apart from every possible angle, and make Megan do it with her. It was as though Megan had to stand in for both Becky *and* Bel, and that meant a lot of listening. It was a relief when the weekend came and Katie was safely away from any note-writing boys.

It was back to normal for this Saturday's football training – no celebrities, just Mrs Ross and a lot of hard work. As usual, Mum dropped Katie off in the car. Katie grabbed her bag and leaned over to give her mum a kiss goodbye.

"See you later, Mum!"

"Hang on, darling, I thought I might come and watch." Mrs Ryan uncoiled herself from the driving seat, and started to root through the junk in the back for her handbag.

Katie stared at her. "Why? It's just normal practice this time, not like last week."

"But it's OK for parents to come and watch, isn't it?" Mum had finally found all her stuff and was locking the car.

"Well, yeah, but you've never wanted to come before."

Katie sometimes felt that it was hard enough getting her family to come to matches, let alone turn up to practice as well. It was one more reason why she really missed Dad – he'd have been there like a shot, but most of the time she just had to make do with his encouraging emails from Egypt. Katie shot several confused looks at Mum as they walked over to the playing fields, but she didn't notice – she seemed to be gazing into space, smiling to herself.

When they reached the pitch, she grinned at Katie. "Hadn't you better go and get ready? Have a good time!" she said as she stationed herself at the edge of the field, and shrugged her scarf up further round her ears.

Katie went off to find Megan and put her boots on, feeling more puzzled than ever.

"Hi Katie! What's your mum doing here?" Megan looked as surprised as Katie had been as she watched Mrs Ryan saying hello to her dad. He quite often came to watch practices — he was very keen on football and loved watching Megan play. The only problem was he tended to get a bit over-excited when (as he saw it) the referee had got it wrong.

"Don't ask me! I was saying goodbye to her like normal and she said she was coming to watch — I nearly died of shock. I mean, let alone that she's never even thought about coming before, it's raining!"

It certainly was — only the most dedicated, football-loving parent would be out on such a grim morning. Katie was distinctly confused. Then it hit her — Mum was probably feeling sorry for her because of the whole Valentine's Day thing! She thought Katie was feeling left out so she was making the effort to come to football. Huh, that must be it. Katie didn't bother explaining this to Megan — it was too embarrassing.

"We'd better go and warm up," she said,

putting irritating parents and sisters to the back of her mind for the moment.

Mrs Ross arrived soon after, carrying a net of footballs and looking pleased with herself. She gathered the team together and explained what they'd be doing – focusing on passing. There was a small groan at this, as passing wasn't exactly the most exciting way to spend the morning, however useful it was. Mrs Ross made a "calm down" gesture with her hands, and smiled round at them.

"OK, OK, I know it's a bit boring, but we're going to finish up the session with a ten minutes each way game with the boys—" There was a chorus of appreciation at this, and the coach grinned. "I thought you'd be pleased. They'll be keen to get their revenge after the fund-raising match last term, so you'll have to do your best. OK! Pairs, please, and let's get on with it."

(The girls had beaten the boys hollow at the fund-raising match, and raised enough money in ticket sales to buy their own, very cool strip, which Annabel had designed.)

Katie was unusually distracted during practice. She couldn't help looking over at Mum every so often, and every time she did it made her feel irritable. About three-quarters of an hour into the session, Katie spotted the boys' squad loping across the field towards them. Mrs Ross had noticed too, and she called the passing exercises to a halt.

"Let's have those balls back, everybody, and then gather round – I need to pick a starting line-up."

Swiftly she picked eleven members of the squad – a bit of a different arrangement, Katie noticed. Obviously Mrs Ross was using the opportunity of a friendly match (well, supposedly) to try out different player combinations. Katie was up front, which was good, though she was paired with Cara Peters, which wasn't so good. Cara was a talented player, but it was hard to think of her as a teammate when she was Amy's best mate, and such a little rat off the pitch. Still, Katie could make the best of it. She'd save up any angst about Cara and take it out on Max – he was being a total prat as usual, gurning at her and Megan as Mr Anderson directed the boys into their positions. Then she grinned. Robin and David had caught her eye and were making the classic "he's crazy!" gesture in perfect unison.

The two teams arranged themselves on the pitch and waited for the starting whistle. Katie took the opportunity to glance over at Mum again. Was she still watching, or had she chickened out and gone to sit in the car, out of the rain? She looked round quickly, and then did a complete double-take. Mum was there all right, but Katie's eyes had flicked straight past her at first because she wasn't where Katie had thought. She'd been expecting to see her still standing next to Megan's dad, but by now dripping wet and flagging. The laughing, chatting couple sharing the huge umbrella was a nasty shock. Mum wasn't even looking at the field – and the tall guy in the raincoat that she was smiling at so flirtily was Max Cooper's dad.

It was unfortunate that Mrs Ross chose just then to blow her whistle for the start of the game. Katie had never been less ready to play a game of football in her life. She was so zoned out that it took Cara's yell of "Katie – get going!" to even start her moving. Katie desperately wrenched her mind away from the pair at the side of the pitch, and tried to concentrate. It was practically impossible. Not only did her eyes seem to be magnetically pulled towards her mum and Mr Cooper – who didn't appear to have noticed there was a problem – but whenever she *was* looking at the pitch, there was Max!

The ten minutes dragged on and Katie just couldn't get into the game. The boys' side were quick to take advantage of the hole in the girls' attack, with Josh Matthews seeming to be here, there and everywhere. He might fancy himself, but he *was* good at football. The boys didn't so much dominate the action as make the girls look as though they were standing still, and at the end of the first half they were two goals up, with only Megan's sterling efforts having kept it from being loads more. As Mrs Ross blew the whistle to change ends, and called out the team changes she wanted to make, Katie was miserably aware that she had never played worse. She wasn't surprised when Mrs Ross took her off, and she was too embarrassed to look at the coach – she knew that Mrs Ross would be wondering what was going on with her.

She trudged off the pitch, dodging the furious glances from her teammates. She jumped as someone suddenly thumped her on the back.

"Thanks, Katie!" Max jeered, grinning. "You played brilliantly – didn't know you'd joined *our* team!"

Katie actually felt like hitting him – or

screaming something along the lines of "What's your stupid dad playing at?", and it was an effort just to walk away. She watched the second half on her own, radiating such gloom that none of the rest of the squad came to see what the matter was. Every so often she sneaked a look at her mum and Mr Cooper. Mum waved cheerfully – she clearly hadn't a clue that Katie had just been substituted for playing the worst match of her life. Katie dropped her eyes to the ground and stared fiercely at the grass. Was something actually going on? She so wished that Megan hadn't said anything last week – she'd probably never have even noticed without her comment! But then Katie's sensible side kicked in, reminding her that it would be even worse if something were going on and she hadn't a clue. . . Wouldn't it? Actually, blissful cluelessness sounded pretty good right now.

Sarah and Cara managed one goal between

them in the second half, but the boys were jubilant at the final whistle, acting like they'd just won the Cup Final or something. The girls trooped silently off the pitch, and still no one spoke to Katie – it was as though she'd been a scapegoat for the whole disaster, even though her bad play in the first half couldn't be blamed for everything. Megan came over and gave her an enquiring, worried look as Mrs Ross called them all together.

"Well, never mind, girls, it was only a friendly!" The coach was trying to sound cheerful. "You'll get them next time, and it's shown us what we need to work on, hasn't it? OK, let's go and get changed."

As Megan and Katie walked over to the changing rooms, Megan was clearly worried, but at the same time she didn't want to make Katie feel worse by asking her why she'd played so badly. Katie could see that her friend just didn't know how to start.

"Sorry I was so useless," she muttered.

"What was wrong?" asked Megan, gratefully seizing the opportunity. "I'm sorry, I know this sounds mean, but it was like your head wasn't in the game at all."

Katie shrugged. "You know what you said last week about Max's dad and my mum looking friendly?"

"Yeah?" Megan looked enquiring.

"And I told you not to be so stupid?"

"Mmmmm. . ." Megan nodded.

Katie sighed a huge and miserable sigh. "I'm not sure you were being that stupid after all. They were standing together watching the game. Didn't you see them? They looked like they were having the time of their lives. What if that's why she came to the practice? To see him?"

"Wow." Megan sounded gobsmacked. "You think that might really be it? What are you going to do?"

"What can I do?" Katie wailed.

"Well, you could ask her!" Megan pointed

out, in a "stating the obvious" tone of voice.

"But I'm not sure if I want to know," Katie said in a small voice.

"Hey Katie!" Running feet sounded behind them, and Robin caught the two girls up. Both Megan and Katie stiffened slightly, waiting for another mean comment about the boys' victory, but Robin smiled at them. "That was bad luck, Katie. Never mind – it was just a practice match."

Katie gave him a very small smile back. "Yeah, I know."

"Um, well, OK! See you on Monday!" He dashed off to the boys' changing rooms, leaving the two girls looking puzzled – but then they had more important things to worry about than the total weirdness of boys. . .

Chapter Six

After last Saturday's practice session, Katie had wanted to talk to Bel and Becky about what she'd thought was just Megan's crazy idea. Suddenly it didn't seem so crazy any more, but now Katie wasn't sure she wanted to talk to her sisters after all. Once Bel was doing her typical overreacting, and Becky was worrying the way she always did, the whole thing would be horribly real. If Katie kept the possibility to herself, she could pretend it wasn't happening – if she tried really hard. But it was difficult not to blurt out her suspicions as soon as she got home – and that was after a practically silent drive home with Mum. Katie hadn't known what to say, so she'd turned the radio on in the end. Luckily Mum seemed to assume she was just down because the practice hadn't gone too well — she *had* gathered that much at least. Thankfully Mum had been on her own, waiting by the gate for Katie. It would have been awful to have to listen to her being nice to Max's dad, especially if they expected her and Max to be nice to each other too.

Katie stomped up the stairs to the triplets' bedroom, trying to banish the picture of her mum smiling up at Max's dad. Becky was sitting on the window seat next to her rats' cage, playing with cinnamon-coloured Fang.

"Hi! How did practice go?"

"Terrible," muttered Katie, gloomily.

Becky, who hadn't really expected any answer but "Fine", possibly followed by a very enthusiastic description to which she would listen with half an ear, looked up from blowing on Fang's whiskers in surprise.

"Why? What went wrong?" She got up and came over to Katie, who was now lying flat on her back on her bed, staring miserably at the ceiling.

"It was a disaster – we had a practice match against the boys and we lost and I played really badly, OK?" Katie snapped out the end of the sentence. She knew none of this was remotely Becky's fault, but she was feeling really upset and angry, and Becky was so terribly easy to be nasty to.

Becky retreated back to the window seat, wisely deciding that her sister didn't want to talk. This left Katie feeling just as cross as before, except now she felt guilty about being horrible to Becky as well. Eventually she heaved herself up off the bed and went upstairs to the attic where they kept the computer. She flumped down on the computer chair, and turned it on, waiting as it chugged through its start-up routine. Eventually she managed to open up her email and it made a sound that was very slightly like applause. Katie clicked her tongue – Bel had been fiddling with the alert sounds again. The email was from Dad, as she'd been hoping – he generally emailed the triplets at the weekend, a separate message for each of them if he could manage it.

Hi Katie!
  Hope everything's going OK, sweetheart. How's the football doing? Scored any more brilliant goals lately? You've got to email me some more pics of you playing – I want to be kept up to date with Manor Hill Junior Girls' world-takeover bid! Things are going pretty well here, we've started building, finally. I'm going to be really sick of this bridge by the time it's up. Still, it'll feel good seeing people using it. I pulled a massive spider out of one of my boots this morning – Bel would have had a fit, especially when Becky wanted to adopt it as a pet. I've attached a picture of me with the foundations for the bridge – I'm the one with the big hat – it's

so hot out here. I've been checking the weather in Darefield on the BBC website – rain, huh? I know you're probably hating it, but it makes me feel really homesick!

Mail me back soon, and tell your mum I said hello.

Loads of love,
Dad

Katie had felt cheered up when she saw the message from Dad, but actually it only made things worse. Katie had hated it so much when her parents split up, and now it seemed like Mum might be thinking about meeting someone new. What was she supposed to say to Dad? And how could she tell him that she'd just messed up really badly in practice when he was so proud of her? She shut down the computer and went to do some more practice against the garden wall.

She did a lot of practice that weekend. Mostly to avoid having to talk to Mum, Becky and Bel. Luckily they all seemed to think that she was going mad on ball-skills because of the disaster on Saturday. Becky and Bel seemed so romance-obsessed that right now Katie felt like she could tell them she was going on a trip to Mars and they'd just ask her to bring them back some chocolate if she went past the corner shop.

Bel had gone to the cinema in town with Josh on Saturday afternoon, and it had gone really well, apparently. He'd held her hand, and she'd spent the rest of the weekend telling every detail to anyone who'd listen – and even those who wouldn't. By Sunday evening Katie was sick to death of Annabel's blissed-out face.

"Did I tell you about the popcorn?" Annabel asked her urgently as Katie walked past her doing her homework (supposedly) in the middle of the stairs.

"*No*," said Katie in the least encouraging way she could. It didn't work.

"Josh bought some—"

"Wow."

Annabel seemed not to have noticed Katie's glower. "And then he did this thing where he chucked a bit of popcorn in the air and then caught it in his mouth. It was so funny!"

"Boring film, then. . ." Katie muttered sarcastically as she stepped over Annabel's history books.

The really annoying thing was that Becky didn't seem to mind Annabel's constant Josh-talk – in fact, she seemed to be encouraging her! Katie knew she couldn't stand Josh either, so why did she keep aahing at all Bel's stories?

It felt strange to be keeping such a massive secret from Bel and Becky, though, even if they were driving her mad. By Monday morning she was desperate to talk it over with someone – she'd emailed Megan over the weekend, but it wasn't really the same as talking it through, and she'd been worried about phoning as there was nowhere really private to do it.

When she got to school on Monday, Sarah, her team captain, was prowling round by the gates, obviously on the lookout for people. Becky nudged Annabel, and they closed in tight behind Katie – they didn't want Sarah having a go at her. Becky had told Annabel about Katie's horrible time at practice, although she'd had difficulty getting a word in edgeways.

Surprisingly, though, Sarah wasn't in too bad a mood.

"Oh good! Look, Katie, we've got an extra practice on Tuesday at lunch – can you tell Megan?"

Katie nodded, feeling relieved. "Sure."

The girls' team had a league match on Wednesday, and Katie guessed that Mrs Ross didn't want them to go into it feeling depressed after the bad session on Saturday. She told Sarah she'd be there, and went off to find Megan. The triplets could see a group of people round the big chestnut tree, so they headed over. Katie realized gloomily when they were closer that it wasn't just Saima, Megan and Fran – in fact, Megan wasn't even in yet. Saima and Fran were chatting to Josh and David, and Josh and David were studiously ignoring each other. Josh seemed to have decided that as Annabel's pretty best friend, Saima was worthy of his attention, but he was behaving as though Fran and David weren't there. Annabel didn't seem to notice this. She tossed back her long hair, pushed one of her butterfly-shaped clips a shade further in, and sauntered over to meet Josh, casting a rather smug glance over her shoulder to see how many people had noticed that she and Josh were together. She was rather hoping that Amy would be around to see.

Yes! Amy was leaning against the fence with Cara a bit further along. Annabel tried not to look too triumphant, but it was hard to resist – she flashed her a quick glance, and was slightly disconcerted by the malevolent glare she got in return. Wow – Amy really was jealous! Annabel grinned to herself – it was so cool being the person that every girl in her year envied! She didn't see Amy and Cara put their heads together and snigger, though. . .

"Hey, Annabel." Josh smiled lazily, and laid an arm over her shoulders.

Katie shuddered. He was like something out of a bad film! She met David's eyes and pulled a sick face at him, which made him snort with laughter that he had to hurriedly disguise as a cough. Luckily Annabel was far too interested in what Josh was saying to notice, although Josh did give Katie and David a sharp look. He was smart enough to know that Katie didn't like him – he just wasn't bothered.

David gave Katie a sympathetic look and went over to Becky, and they and Fran wandered off.

Josh smiled nastily at Katie. "So, I heard there's an extra practice for your lot tomorrow then?"

Katie shrugged. "Yeah."

Josh just smirked, like he knew something she didn't. Then he turned his back on her and steered Annabel with him – Katie was abandoned again.

"Have you had any more of those notes?" Megan asked, as they sat eating their lunch in the dining hall. The others were all in the art room, so it was safe to discuss Katie's secret admirer problem.

"No, thank goodness. Maybe whoever it was has forgotten about it," said Katie hopefully. She knew it wasn't likely, but still. . . She had enough to worry about just now. She was really nervous about the lunchtime practice the next day, and it niggled at her all through school, and the next morning as well. OK, so Sarah didn't seem to be holding a grudge, but most of the Year Eights in the team were complete fair-weather friends. They loved Katie when she was scoring the goals for them, but when she or Megan or Cara did anything wrong, they were "those dumb Year Sevens". And Cara wasn't exactly holding back either. She and Amy and Emily kept very obviously stifling sniggers every time they saw Katie, and darting nasty, significant little smiles at Annabel for some reason as well.

As it turned out, Katie did get a few dirty looks, but the girls had more to worry about than getting at her. Shortly after they got on to the pitch, they had visitors. The first Katie knew of it was the little frown that developed between Mrs Ross's eyebrows as she was explaining the warm-up exercises she wanted them to do. The coach seemed to be staring at something over the girls' shoulders. Katie cast a quick look back, and drew in a sharp breath.

Most of the boys' squad (David and Robin were notable exceptions) were lined up along the side of the pitch, smiling – nastily. Like they were trying to give the girls a message.

Josh, of course, was right in the middle, and Max was there too, grinning his face off at Katie. The thing was, it was difficult for Mrs Ross to send them away. Friends quite often came to watch practices – in fact, Amy and Emily were taking advantage of a rare spell of sunshine at the side of the pitch as well, in theory watching Cara, but more just gossiping.

It was very difficult to do exercises and work on tactics while fifteen boys were watching you like hyenas circling a wounded animal. Soon everyone was making stupid mistakes, and Mrs Ross looked like she was considering telling the boys to get lost – that would be really embarrassing!

"Look!" It was Megan, hissing over her shoulder as she dribbled a ball past Katie. "Over there!"

Katie looked almost reluctantly – Megan's face had been worried, and she wasn't sure she could cope with more stuff going wrong. She saw immediately what Megan had meant. Amy wasn't standing next to Emily any more, and she certainly wasn't watching Cara. Demurely fiddling with a lock of her long strawberry-blonde hair, she was gazing up at Josh Matthews as though she thought he was the most interesting person in the world, and batting her eyelashes at him. And Josh was positively lapping it up. As Katie watched, he smirked at Amy, and put an arm round her shoulders – just like he'd done with Annabel the day before!

Katie had to concentrate very hard to avoid a repeat of Saturday's dreadful performance. Thoughts were racing through her head – that she had been right all along, that Josh was a two-timing snake. . .

Mrs Ross drew the agonizing practice to a close and they had to run the gauntlet of the boys to get back into school and change – but Katie couldn't care less about their jeering remarks.

"Well spotted," she muttered bitterly to

Megan, storming ahead. "I knew it! But Amy? Wow, I thought he had better taste than that."

"Scary, isn't it?" Megan agreed.

"What am I going to say to Bel? That's the real problem," Katie groaned. "She's not going to believe me – she thinks the sun shines out of his eyes."

Megan looked thoughtful. "You know, I'm not sure you should say anything to her."

Katie turned round in shock. "What? I can't just leave it!"

Megan stopped walking and folded her arms, forcing Katie to come back to her reluctantly. "You can, you know. Bel can sort herself out. You and Becky have said loads of times that you think Josh is bad news, and she's never believed you. You're just going to have to let her work it out. Sooner or later she'll realize."

"But – " Katie got that far and stopped. She could see Megan was making sense, it was just so against her nature to abandon Annabel to her fate – she *always* rescued her sisters. Megan was right though – sometimes there was no telling Annabel – especially when it came to her specialist subject – boys. And it wasn't as if Katie could *prove* he'd been flirting with Amy – if Annabel asked him he'd probably just say that he couldn't get rid of her. Josh was easily smart enough to come up with a story on the spot.

Katie sighed. Megan was right – maybe she had to let it go. And that meant that she just had to wait for everything to go wrong for Annabel. . .

Chapter Seven

It was so difficult for Katie to watch Annabel and Josh together and not say anything. She didn't think that he'd spotted her and Megan watching him with Amy, but maybe he had and he just didn't care? He turned up to chat to Annabel in the bit of lunch that was left after the practice, and he seemed to be smirking whenever Katie looked at him (which was as little as possible). Several times that afternoon Katie nearly blurted out what she'd seen, but something always stopped her. Generally it was the blissful expression on Bel's face as she daydreamed her way through lessons. It was not the face of someone who wanted to be told that their boyfriend was a louse.

When they got home on Tuesday night she did tell Becky, who wasn't at all surprised.

"Poor Bel! That's so awful, she'll be gutted! David's always said how mean Josh is, but I never thought he'd do something like that."

A flash of irritation lit up in Katie. Honestly! Didn't Becky even *think* without David these days? But Becky didn't seem to notice. She *was* surprised that Katie didn't want to tell Annabel what was going on, though.

"But we have to tell her!" she said, stroking one of her bunches against her cheek worriedly. "We have to, Katie! We can't let her go on thinking how wonderful he is, that's not fair!"

Katie shrugged. Megan's common sense had worked on her by now, however much she didn't want it to. "You tell her then."

Becky put the end of her hair in her mouth, and chewed it, her eyes panicky.

"Becky, there's no point in telling her, because she just won't believe us, and we'll only make her upset — and angry with us too. And if she's not talking to us there'll be nobody to help her sort it out when it all goes pear-shaped. All Josh actually did was talk to Amy — and put his arm round her. I mean, you could see they were flirting, but we can't prove it."

"I can't believe you're so calm about this." Becky sounded quite hurt — it seemed almost as if Katie didn't care.

Katie sighed exasperatedly. "I'm not calm! I wanted to go and throttle him, and that rat Amy! But I talked about it with Megan after practice, and she made me see that there was no point trying to rescue Bel when she doesn't want to be rescued. We just have to wait."

Becky managed to look even more hurt — she did that trick where her eyes seemed to be swimming in tears, which in Katie's current mood just made her want to throttle Becky as well as Josh and Amy.

"Don't look at me like that! Megan was there

and you weren't. You were probably painting hearts with David, or talking to David, or thinking about *David*."

Katie glared at her sister and stomped out of the room, starting to feel really, really guilty before she'd even got to the door. . .

Becky clearly felt that she'd been letting Katie down – she was very good at assuming things were her fault, and she'd taken her sister's outburst to heart. She didn't (surprise, surprise) take it on herself to say anything to Annabel, though she did look edgy and worried when her sister started trying to decide exactly which film stars Josh looked most like. They'd been doing their homework, her and Katie at the big table in their room, and Annabel on the stairs. Annabel had rushed into the bedroom with a piece of paper, one that she was waving far too excitedly for it to be her science homework. It turned out that she'd adapted the flow chart they were supposed to be producing to detail all the features of the various actors, and then work out whose nose Josh had. She was disappointed in the lack of enthusiasm from Katie and Becky.

"I was going to cut out the different bits of the faces from magazines and everything," she finished grumpily. "What are you two looking so miserable for?"

"We're doing homework, Bel," muttered Katie irritably, and Annabel sighed in disgust, grabbed a couple of magazines and a pair of scissors, and vanished in a twirl of flounced denim skirt.

"You're right."

Katie glanced up from the proper kind of flow chart again. "What?"

"I'm saying that I'm sorry, you're right about her and Josh." Becky gazed hopefully at her with her huge dark-blue eyes. "And I'm sorry I've been hanging around with David so much, I didn't realize it was getting to you."

"Not getting to me," Katie muttered, feeling ashamed of herself. "David's really nice. I'm sorry."

"Anyway, I'm going to be more thoughtful from now on – I feel really bad. Fran's probably sick of me being with David all the time as well, and I didn't even realize!"

Katie sighed. "I bet she isn't. I'm just being grumpy because I'm worried about Bel. And – well, other stuff."

She looked thoughtfully at Becky and considered telling her sister about her suspicions to do with Mum and Mr Cooper. But she really didn't want to have the same conversation all over again – this time about Mum and Max's dad instead of Josh and Annabel. And she could just imagine Becky's reaction. Panic, loads of questions as Becky tried to get her head round the idea, and general fuss and bother. She shuddered slightly. She just didn't feel like dealing with that right now.

Becky raised an eyebrow enquiringly, and Katie had to think of something:

"You know, football – I'm still really cross about how badly I did at that practice on Saturday, and I think everyone else in the team is going to hold it against me for ages. Mrs Ross has still picked me for tomorrow's match, but she easily might not have done. I've got to be really careful, play extra well."

Becky nodded understandingly, and reached over to pat her arm. "Don't worry – you will. You always pull it off in the end, don't you?" She smiled encouragingly, but despite Becky's trust in her, Katie was left feeling that this time she was up to her neck in a whole load of complicated stuff that she just might not be able to sort out.

It didn't help that Mum was definitely being a bit weird. She was even more forgetful than usual and a couple of times Katie had noticed her on the phone being quite giggly and smiley.

She seemed to be really entering in to the whole Valentine's Day thing, as well, and on Wednesday at breakfast she even asked Katie whether she wanted some heart-shaped cakes for the sleepover party.

"Mum! It's meant to be an anti-Valentine's Day party! Of course I don't want heart-shaped cakes!"

"Oh yes, darling, I'm sorry, I forgot for a minute." Mum smiled vaguely at her.

"So what kind of cakes *do* you want?" Annabel asked, in a rather patronizing voice. "Footballs?" She sniggered into her cereal.

Katie scowled. "How about we make some heart-shaped ones and tear them in half," she growled. Then she slapped her toast down on the plate and went out to get her books ready for school, leaving the rest of her family staring after her in surprise.

Katie's walk to school could just about be described as with her sisters, but only loosely.

She stalked about five metres ahead of them the whole way — and that set the tone for the rest of the day.

"Have you had a fight with Becky and Bel?" Megan asked as they were changing into their kit after school.

"Not really. It's just like our entire house is being taken over by Valentine's Day and I got a bit annoyed about it at breakfast. Why?"

"Ummm, I don't know. They haven't spoken to you much all day. And they keep looking at you as though you're a bomb that might go off any minute."

"Huh. Well, I feel a bit like that. I've got too many things I'm not telling too many people. It's horrible." Katie paused. "You do know how grateful I am to you for putting up with my moaning, don't you?" she added, smiling a bit shamefacedly.

Megan just grinned at her. "It's fine — don't start stressing about that as well."

Katie grinned back, relieved. "I tell you

what though, I'm really looking forward to this game." She slammed her locker door shut so hard that the whole row shuddered, and the rest of the team, scattered round the changing rooms, stared at her. She giggled. St Luke's had better watch out!"

St Luke's certainly weren't prepared for the avenging angel that was Katie Ryan that afternoon. And the rest of her team looked a bit bemused as well. It wasn't that Katie was playing selfishly – Sarah and Cara still got plenty of time with the ball – but somehow, whenever the play was up front, Katie seemed to be in exactly the right place at the right time with a very determined expression on her face. By half–time Manor Hill were three goals up, and the St Luke's team were displaying a range of grimaces from confused to upset via very, very sulky.

"Wow!" Megan handed Katie a cup of orange squash and grinned at her. "I should think you need that. Two goals! *And* setting that one up for Sarah! Can we get you really annoyed before all the league matches? I haven't had to do anything; I felt like leaning on the goalpost and having a snooze."

Mrs Ross happened to be right behind Megan, to hear this, unfortunately, but thankfully she didn't take it too seriously. She did decide it was time for a team pep-talk though.

"Right, listen up everybody! You've played brilliantly today – so far. But please don't go getting too complacent. I know the St Luke's coach and she's very good. Right this minute she's going to be telling her team that they need to pull out all the stops, and they're going to come back on the field desperate to claw back some goals. If you're not careful you could be in trouble – just remember that if we can score three goals in a half, so can they, and then they'd be just one away from winning. So, concentrate please, all of you!" Mrs Ross waited until the girls were all chatting amongst themselves again, and then sought out Katie, who was smiling happily into her squash. Seeing the coach coming she tried very hard to assume the expression of somebody who was not in the slightest bit complacent.

"Well done, Katie! That was brilliant, two great goals – and I was really pleased with the goal you set up for Sarah as well. It's great to see you girls playing for the team rather than trying to get goals for yourselves. Really good!"

The second half was as Mrs Ross had predicted – St Luke's were desperate. But they were so desperate that they were flailing about all over the place. Katie, watching one of their forwards lose possession to Cara through a silly mistake, felt like telling them just to calm down a bit, to stand back and think instead of running frantically after the ball with no idea what they were going to do with it if they got it.

When they shook hands at the end of the game, Manor Hill were celebrating a four-nil win. At least something was going right, finally! The St Luke's team climbed dismally into their minibus, and the Manor Hill girls headed off to change again.

Katie was changed in double-quick time, eager to get off and meet Mum and tell her how brilliantly the match had gone. While she was waiting for Megan to get her socks on, she rooted round in the front of her rucksack for her lip balm, a present from Annabel that she *did* actually use.

"Oh no." Katie's voice sounded almost frightened.

Megan, who was hopping on one leg as she pulled her sock on, looked up in surprise and tried not to overbalance. "What's the matter?"

Katie pulled a familiar-looking piece of paper out of the pocket of her bag. "Look – another one." She was holding it as though she expected it to bite her.

"Aren't you going to read it?" Megan asked interestedly.

"I suppose so – I'd rather just throw it away. It might tell me who it's from though, I guess." She unfolded the piece of paper gingerly.

SEE YOU AT THE VALENTINE'S BALL!
WILL YOU DANCE WITH ME?

Katie handed it to Megan. "Another good reason not to go to that thing," she said disgustedly. "But Becky and Bel made me promise."

"Still no clue who it's from?" Megan peered over Katie's shoulder at the note.

"Nope – anyone could know I'm going to the ball. Bel's been going on about it every time she's opened her mouth for the last week. What am I going to do? I'd almost forgotten about the last note, it was more than a week ago now. I was hoping whoever it was had given up or something."

"So at least you'll probably find out who it is at the dance," said Megan thoughtfully.

"Great," Katie muttered. "Then I just have to tell them to get lost. That'll be fun."

The note put a damper on Katie's excitement over the victory, and she trailed out to the car not looking like someone who'd scored two goals and been instrumental in two more.

Mum saw her coming and put on a sympathetic face. "How did it go?"

"Oh, we won. I scored two goals. What's for tea?"

Mrs Ryan looked slightly blank. She'd had understanding and reassuring mother all prepared, and now the wind had been taken out of her sails rather. "Ummm, fish pie. Er, is everything all right? Did you have an argument with Megan?"

Katie looked thoughtfully at her mother. Was everything all right? Huh. How would Mum react if she told her what was really on her mind: "Well, I think Bel's boyfriend is two-timing her with one of our worst enemies, some idiot's been sending me lovenotes and I haven't a clue who it is, and I think you might be going to date the father of the boy who deliberately crippled me last term. Hmmm, so no, not really."

Maybe it wasn't a very good idea. . .

Chapter Eight

Katie decided that she just had to slog through Thursday and Friday at school. It was so hard to be normal when she felt like she was holding so much back from the people she usually confided in. At least by the end of Friday evening one of her problems should be solved, although it wasn't going to be much fun doing it. How *did* you tell somebody who'd been sending you love letters that you just weren't interested? Katie was almost tempted to ask Annabel, but she seemed to be following Josh around all the time at school, and at home she was obviously just daydreaming about the next time she saw him – Katie wasn't sure any advice from her would be worth much right now. Even Becky and Saima were getting a bit tired of Annabel's one topic of conversation. Maybe the sleepover on Saturday would be a good time to sound out Bel about how she reckoned everything was going with him. After all, how long was Katie supposed to let her go on being messed around?

As for the whole Mum thing, Katie hadn't got a clue what to do. She'd noticed that Max had been behaving a bit weirdly recently. Could he have guessed what was going on as well? In geography on Friday afternoon she caught him staring at her with a really strange expression on his face. She was used to him giving her evil looks, or sneering at her, but this was different. He looked almost frightened, and when he realized she'd noticed him he ducked his head right down and stared at his book for the next ten minutes without looking up. There was no way that was normal Max behaviour. Katie felt even more worried. When it was just her and Megan with vague suspicions the whole idea had been horrible, but not very real. But if Max had noticed too. . .

At the end of school that afternoon there was a noticeable air of excitement as people raced home to get changed. But Katie really wasn't in the best place for an Annabel-style makeover. It wasn't something she enjoyed much at the best of times, and right now she felt that looking as unattractive as possible for this party would be a good idea. She flatly refused to let Annabel curl her hair.

"Why not?" Annabel wailed. She'd curled her own hair and was looking particularly sophisticated. Katie guessed she was trying to look older for Josh's sake. "Please tell me you're not just going to stick it in a ponytail? How boring can you get? You have to make a bit of an effort, Katie!"

"Why?" Katie growled. "I don't want to go! It's going to be embarrassing and horrible."

Becky turned round from the mirror where

she was holding up tops against her favourite jeans to find the best combination. She really wanted David to be impressed, and the good thing about having two identical sisters was having the run of three wardrobes when you most needed it. "Katie, it's just a party! Why should it be embarrassing?"

Suddenly the pressure of secrets was too much. Although she'd decided that she wasn't going to, Katie just *had* to tell Becky and Annabel about the notes – she needed them to help her survive the evening.

She got up from her bed and went to grab her rucksack. "Listen Bel, you have to promise me that you're not going to go mad over this, OK?"

Annabel pricked up her ears. This sounded *interesting*. Becky put down the current outfit she was considering and came to stand next to Annabel.

Katie pulled the two notes out of her rucksack pocket and spread them out on the bed. Then she stood back and waited for the explosion.

Annabel grabbed the first one, and wheeled round clutching it. "Somebody sent this to *you*."

Katie suddenly saw the funny side, which she'd been totally missing up until now. Maybe it was Annabel's incredulous face, maybe it was the relief of sharing this whole weird thing with her sisters. "There's no need to sound quite that surprised," she said, mock-insulted.

"Katie, this is so cool!" Annabel was practically jumping up and down with excitement.

"Bel, you promised! It's not cool! I don't want anybody to fancy me. I'm quite happy not having a boyfriend!" Katie glared at them both – even Becky was looking far too enthusiastic.

"Yes, yes, yes, I know that, you're *always* saying so. But it's still nice to be liked, Katie!

Do you know who they're from?" Annabel compared the writing on the two notes carefully.

"No – but I'm going to find out tonight, aren't I? *That's* why it's all going to be so embarrassing!"

"We can help," Becky suggested. "If we stay close to you, then we can rescue you if it does get really embarrassing."

Katie smiled gratefully. For once maybe it would be nice to be the one who was being rescued.

"But this means that you have to look extra-good," Annabel put in firmly, pushing Katie on to a chair and grabbing her curling wand.

"Why?" Both Katie and Becky sounded confused.

"Because it's much easier to do difficult stuff like this when you know you look good. C'mon, take that hairband out."

Katie sighed and pulled off the band, shaking her long hair free. "Just don't take too long, OK? Only do a few bits or something, I'm not sitting still for hours."

"Fine, fine. Look, I'll put it up for you, OK? Like this—" Annabel riffled through a magazine and waved a picture at Katie. "Topknots, yes?"

Katie scowled at the picture, but surprisingly it wasn't too bad. She quite liked the look of the model's hair – it didn't look as though it was going to fall apart as soon as she moved, for a start.

"OK."

"Have you decided what you're going to wear?" Becky asked thoughtfully. Katie was currently modelling a highly attractive dressing gown.

"No. Look, you might as well just tell me. I'm going to end up wearing what you two want anyway, aren't I?" Now that she'd agreed to let the other two help her, she felt as though a weight had been lifted off her shoulders – it was nice to let somebody else make all the decisions for once. "Just nothing too pink, OK?"

Annabel smiled happily. It was good to have Katie behaving sensibly – it didn't happen often. "Uh-huh. Well, I reckon you should wear my blue dress. The stripy one? It's quite sporty, so it should look really good on you."

Katie made a face, but more because she felt that Becky and Annabel expected it of her than because she actually objected to the dress. Annabel was right, if she had to wear a dress, that one was a lot better than some they could have tried to force her into. Feeling vaguely as though she was winning, she allowed Annabel to do her eye make-up, though she did make a stand on nail polish.

"No. You know I can't sit still for long enough, Bel, and then it gets scuffed and I have to take it off because it drives me mad that it's spoilt. There's no point unless you're going to tie me up to start with."

Annabel looked as though the idea was

tempting, but she still had her own make-up to do, and Becky's to sort out once her sister had admitted that she'd done it all wrong, so she gave in. "Oh, OK. I suppose there isn't really time anyway. I've got to look really good – I need to impress Josh and his mates."

Katie sighed. Bel really was completely entranced by that idiot.

Annabel was still applying mascara for Becky when Mum called up the stairs that they needed to go.

"Sit still! We don't want to be dead on time, that would be really sad. Katie, go and tell Mum we're nearly ready."

Katie disappeared downstairs obediently. It was quite restful not being the bossy sister for once, but she wondered how long that would last. She had a feeling that it wouldn't take her *very* long to get sick of it.

The school hall looked fantastic. Becky and Annabel gazed round proudly as they walked in – it had looked fab at lunchtime when they'd finished putting up the decorations, but now it was dark outside and the hall was full of people it looked loads better. Even Katie could see how much work they'd put into it.

"Wow – it looks so different. Did you make all of this stuff?"

Becky nodded. "Mm–hm. Us and Saima and Fran and David. And Mrs Cranmer, of course. Me and David mostly just did those big pink hearts, Bel and Fran did the complicated bits."

The pink hearts were holding up swags of white and silver streamers that ran all round the walls, and Katie decided that by complicated bits Becky meant the little cupids that were dotted round the walls in a variety of poses.

"Saima made all those roses round the tables," Annabel put in. "She learned how to make them from one of her cousins, I think. They had a big engagement party for her auntie and they hired a hall and decorated it."

Groups of people were dotted round the hall, but no one was dancing yet, even though the music was on. And it was very noticeable that no one was mixing with people from other classes – all the Year Sevens were gathering over in the corner by the stage.

Annabel dashed over to Saima. "Hey! You look fantastic – I thought you were going to wear your pink trousers!"

Saima stroked the lilac silk of her sari complacently. "Well, I was, but then I decided it would be more fun to wear this. My grandmother sent it for my birthday. I hardly ever wear my Indian clothes, only for family parties and stuff, but they're fun if you really feel like dressing up. And I did!"

Annabel looked enviously at the gorgeous material, and the pretty little purple top that Saima was wearing underneath the sari – she looked like a model, and loads of the Year Seven boys kept shooting her admiring glances.

"Josh came looking for you, by the way. I told him you'd be here soon."

"Oh, OK." Annabel looked round for Josh hopefully, but couldn't spot him. "He'll turn up," she said, sounding more casual than she felt.

Saima grinned at her – she knew perfectly well that Annabel was putting it on. "Anyway, you look great, too. And I can't believe you got Katie to wear a dress!" Saima waved at Becky and Katie, who were talking to Fran.

"Oooh, I nearly forgot! You'll never guess what's been happening!" Annabel filled Saima in on the whole secret admirer thing. Katie had said she supposed she didn't mind them telling Saima and Fran and David, as long as no one went on about it.

"So we have to look out for him, OK?"

"Definitely! This is so exciting!" Saima stared interestedly round the hall, as though she expected someone to appear with a sign saying "Katie's Mystery Admirer".

Annabel gazed round, still hunting for Josh. "Listen, Saima, I've just got to go to the loo. Back in a sec, OK?"

Saima shrugged and went to talk to David and Becky.

Annabel made her way to the girls' toilets which were outside the hall. She was walking back down the corridor when she spotted Josh. Unfortunately, he didn't see her, which perhaps explained why he was sitting on one of the corridor windowsills with Amy Mannering.

Josh had his arm around Amy and she was giggling as he whispered something to her. Just then Amy looked up and saw Annabel, who was frozen to the spot. Josh followed her gaze and smirked when he saw Annabel's frosty glare.

She looked down her nose disgustedly, and said, in a voice that was impressively un-trembly. "Congratulations, Josh – you've finally found your perfect match. She's just as slimy as you are."

Then she stalked off back to the hall, refusing even to sniff until she'd got round the corner.

She wasn't sure quite what to say to the others, but it turned out she didn't need to say anything. She walked up to Katie, who was chatting with Megan. Katie took one look at Annabel's face and burst out, "Oh Bel! What did he do?"

"He was with Amy – Amy!" Annabel hissed.

Katie put an arm round her, and Megan gave her a sympathetic look – then she turned round to see if the others were near. She reckoned Annabel could do with both her sisters right now. Becky caught her eye, took one look at Annabel, and skidded up looking worried. She threw her arms round Bel.

"Don't make me cry. I don't want to give Josh the satisfaction. You were right about him, Katie – he's a worm."

"Mmmm – I'm really sorry, Bel, I wish I hadn't been."

"I can't believe it – he was so *nice* to me! He can't have meant a word of it."

"Um, hi?" came a voice from behind them, and the girls looked round – whoever this was, their timing was awful.

The tall good-looking boy smiled warmly. "Hey, Annabel . . . I was just wondering if you wanted to dance."

Annabel looked thoughtful – it was Dan Mitchell from Year Eight. He'd been Buttons in the play and had always seemed really nice. Not to mention *very* good-looking, and after all, the best way to show Josh she didn't care about him and Amy would be to find somebody else.

She smiled determinedly at Dan. "Sure. That would be nice." But as she followed him on to the dance floor she muttered in Katie's ear, "Don't worry, I won't believe a word he says. . ."

The drama with Josh had totally put Katie's secret admirer problem out of the triplets' heads. Becky and David went to dance, and Katie wandered over to the drinks table with Megan, still keeping half an eye on Annabel, and another half on Josh and Amy, who were also dancing. Josh looked distinctly disappointed that he'd been done out of a tearful ex-girlfriend scene, and Katie wouldn't have put it past him to try something else.

They walked past a group of boys from their class, and Robin called out, "Hey, Katie!" He left his mates and walked over to the drinks table with her and Megan. "Is Bel OK? I thought she was seeing Josh Matthews?"

"So did Bel." Katie shrugged. "He's a worm, what can I say?"

"Wow, that's really awful. Hey, do you want to dance?"

Katie had come to the party with the express intention of not dancing with anyone, but Robin was a mate. She could get a drink later. She looked enquiringly at Megan – she didn't want to abandon her.

"Mmm, you go, I'm desperate for something to drink. See you in a bit."

"OK. I like this one."

They headed over to where Becky and David were dancing. Robin was a surprisingly good dancer and Katie was enjoying herself – until something suddenly clicked in her mind.

She looked thoughtfully at him, and he went pink. Katie did a mental run-through of the last few times she'd spoken to Robin. Him being so nice after the disastrous practice . . . asking if she was going to the Valentine's Ball. . . She stopped dancing, and so did Robin, and they stared at each other, oblivious to everyone still laughing and talking around them.

"It was you!" Katie breathed, shocked.

Robin was blushing scarlet by now. He coughed. "Look, can we get out of here?" He gave her a pleading look and nodded at everyone dancing, and they shuffled their way through the other dancers to the edge of the room.

"It was you, wasn't it? You sent me those notes?"

"Um, yeah. . . I wasn't sure what you'd say if I asked you for real. I do really like you, you know. I wasn't trying to freak you out or anything."

"It was really weird!"

"Sorry! I was hoping you'd be pleased – with it being Valentine's Day coming up and everything. I thought girls liked that kind of stuff." Robin looked miserable.

Katie sighed. "I'm sorry, Robin. The notes were sweet – it was romantic, I suppose, but I'm not feeling very into that kind of thing right now." She took a deep breath, and tried to think of all the tips for telling people you weren't interested that Annabel had given her while she was doing her hair. "Can't we just be friends? Please? I mean, you're a mate."

Robin's miserable expression lifted slightly. "Yeah? That's good. I mean, if we can't go out, at least you're still talking to me."

"Course." Katie nodded. "And if you ever want to meet up and kick a ball about in the park, that'd be cool."

"OK." Robin seemed almost relieved.

Katie looked round at the dance floor – Annabel still dancing with Dan, smiling at him and looking really happy; Becky whispering something in David's ear. It looked fun.

She smiled at Robin. "Want to finish that dance?"

Chapter Nine

"I still can't believe it was Robin!" Annabel said, shaking her head. "I mean, *Robin*? Sending you secret notes? It's so strange! I thought it would be somebody we didn't really know."

"Sorry!" Katie grinned, and shrugged. She couldn't believe how much better she felt now that she no longer had to worry about her mystery admirer, or that slime ball Josh.

For once, all three of the triplets were up early (ish) on Saturday morning. Annabel and Becky were both keen to get the post as soon as it arrived, and they'd dragged Katie downstairs with them. They were all sitting round the kitchen table in their onesies, discussing the events of the night before.

"It was a really fun party in the end," Katie went on thoughtfully. "OK, so I don't want to go out with Robin, but he's a very good dancer. Maybe it's something to do with being good at football. Fancy footwork and everything."

Annabel shook her head. "No mention of footballers allowed, it reminds me of you-know-who."

"*Dan* doesn't play football then?" Becky giggled.

Annabel looked haughty. "Actually no. He thinks ice-hockey is much more demanding. He says football's all just luck, no skill involved."

Katie spluttered into her cornflakes. "Oh, does he? Are you going out with this idiot then?"

Annabel looked thoughtful. "Maybe – maybe not. He talked about himself an awful lot, and Josh did that. I reckon it's a bad sign. I'll have to see."

Katie raised her eyebrows at Becky. It

sounded as though Annabel was actually being sensible about a boy for once, instead of being dazzled by a good-looking face.

Mum was making herself a cup of coffee, but Katie noticed that she seemed to be a bit jittery. She kept peering round at the kitchen clock, and then leaning over towards the door as though she was listening for something. It wasn't until Katie looked back to the table and saw that Becky and Annabel were doing pretty much the same thing that she realized what was going on. Mum was waiting for the post too! Katie sighed. With all the drama yesterday evening, she'd almost forgotten about Mum and Max's dad, but it looked as if something really *was* going on there, if Mum was expecting a card. Katie couldn't remember her having one before, not since – well, not since she and Dad had split up.

Somehow all Katie's appetite for cornflakes had disappeared. She poked dismally at her bowl and started listening too – except she was dreading the arrival of the post.

Annabel suddenly perked up. "What was that? Was that the letterbox?"

There had definitely been a clink, and now they heard the soft fluttery thump of envelopes falling on the mat – *lots* of envelopes.

"I'll go," squeaked Annabel unnecessarily, as she was already halfway out of the door.

"Why's she getting so excited?" growled Katie. "Dan can't have sent her a card already, surely!"

"I think she's got a bet on with Saima, about who gets the most cards," Becky explained, but Katie wasn't really listening, she was watching Mum, who was trying hard to look relaxed, but nibbling her thumbnail like Becky did when she was worried. She met Katie's eyes and looked guilty, then swallowed a massive gulp of coffee, and choked.

Annabel came back into the kitchen, counting envelopes, to find Mum bent double and spluttering, Katie scowling like a really irritable gargoyle, and Becky clearly thinking that she'd missed something somewhere.

"Six for me, three for Becky, two for you, Katie, and one that some idiot's addressed wrong – it says S Ryan, someone's got one of our names wrong. Can I count it for me in my bet with Saima, do you think? I mean, it's bound to be for me really, isn't it?" She gazed hopefully round at Becky and Katie and encountered the scowl.

"What's that look for?" she asked, surprised. "It *is* bound to be for me!"

Katie reached out and plucked the offending card, in a pretty silvery envelope, from Annabel's hand, and handed it to her mother. "S is for Sue, Bel. It's a card for Mum."

Then she walked out of the kitchen.

Annabel stared after her, then looked back at the card, which her mother was holding as though she thought it might bite her. "It's for you?" She sounded incredulous.

Mrs Ryan gave her a rather small smile. "It is possible you know, Bel."

"Aren't you going to open it?" Becky asked, staring at the card.

"Later," said Mrs Ryan, firmly. Which clearly meant, *When you aren't here*.

Annabel and Becky exchanged indignant glances. Katie obviously knew more about this than they did – she'd been holding out on them!

"I think we'll go and open these upstairs," said Annabel, equally firmly. "C'mon, Becky."

As they headed for the stairs, Becky looked back through the kitchen door, to see Mum sit down at the table, and stare at the card as though she still couldn't quite believe it was there. . .

Annabel dashed into the triplets' bedroom. "Katie! What's going on? Who's sent Mum a Valentine's Day card?"

"Not sure," muttered Katie, who was lying on

her bed with a football magazine in front of her. She was still somehow hoping that this was all a big misunderstanding, and she wanted to put off admitting the truth for as long as possible. The magazine might as well have been upside down for all the use she was getting out of it, but she'd known that Annabel and Becky were bound to follow her upstairs, and she wanted some camouflage.

For once, Annabel wasn't that interested in her own love life. She dumped the pile of cards on the table, and stood in front of Katie, arms folded and looking grim.

"You *knew* about this," she stated accusingly.

"Didn't really," Katie muttered again, still gazing at a feature on David Beckham.

Annabel huffed, and snatched the magazine from under her sister's nose. "Stop messing about! You *do* know what's going on, or you wouldn't have sulked out of the kitchen like that – so talk. Who's the card from?"

Katie sighed. Hiding her head in the sand –

like she'd been trying to for a fortnight – just wasn't going to work. She had to face up to what was going on. She propped her chin on her hands, and looked up at her sisters for the first time. "I think it might – *might,* Bel – be from Mr Cooper."

Annabel looked blank. "Who's he?"

Becky gasped in horror as she realized the significance of the name, and Annabel wheeled round on her. "Who is he? Come on, one of you, tell me!"

Katie smiled at her, grimly enjoying passing on the bad news. "Mr Cooper – Jeff Cooper – *Max* Cooper's dad." Then she watched Annabel's expression change from intense curiosity to complete horror.

"No!"

"Oh yes." Katie nodded, still with the grim smile.

"Why on earth would he send Mum a Valentine's card? They don't even know each other – except that she phoned him up to have a go about Max!" Annabel sounded disbelieving.

Katie shrugged. "They met at football practice."

"And anyway, how do you know about all this? And why haven't you told us?" Annabel had recovered from the shock and was back on the attack.

Katie sat up crossly. "When was I supposed to tell you? When you were murmuring sweet nothings to Josh, maybe? When you were both decorating the hall for that party? When Becky and David were shopping for fluffy toy animals? Or when you were all discussing the best outfits for the party, the right make-up for the party, the proper shoes to wear for the party. . . I haven't been able to get a word in edgeways for weeks! I was worrying about you and Josh, trying to work out who was sending me those notes, *and* stressing about Mum, and I couldn't talk to you two about any of it."

"You could!" protested Becky, looking hurt.

Katie sighed. "Well, it didn't feel like I could. I talked to Megan instead. It was her that first pointed out Mum and Mr Cooper anyway, she spotted them chatting at that football masterclass we had."

"I can't believe this," muttered Annabel. "Mum and Max's dad. It's a nightmare. No wonder you've been grumpy for the last couple of weeks—"

"Thanks!" Katie snapped.

"Well, you have, but I'm saying you had an excuse! I thought you were just being sulky because of me and Becky having boyfriends when you didn't."

Surprisingly, it was Becky who reacted to this, as Katie was too cross to get her answer out at once. "Bel! That's so unfair! Katie's just *said* that she couldn't talk to us about all the stuff that was going on because we were so wrapped up in boys and everything. You'd be grumpy, trying to deal with things like that on your own! I'm really sorry, Katie."

Annabel sighed exasperatedly and rolled her eyes to the ceiling. Then she shrugged, flopped down next to Katie on the bed and gave her a hug. "Oh, OK, I'm sorry too. You still should have told us about Max's dad though!" she added. "I can't believe you didn't!"

"I just wasn't sure," Katie explained. "And I didn't want to believe it, either. If I'd told you two it would have been like a *real* thing, do you see what I mean? Now we all know, I can't tell myself I'm imagining it any more."

"What are we going to do?" asked Becky, curling up next to them on the bed.

"I don't think we *can* do anything," said Katie. "If they're going to go out then they're going to go out. They can't make us be nice to Max, though," she added viciously.

The other two nodded firmly. No way. But then Becky thought of something. "Does he know, do you think?"

"I reckon he might." Katie nodded. "He was giving me this really odd look yesterday; he seemed totally miserable."

"Maybe he is," Becky wondered.

Annabel raised her eyebrows, and Becky shrugged. "Well, it's even worse for him, isn't it? I mean, we've still *got* Dad, even if he's in Egypt. But it's just Max and his dad, so sharing him with somebody must be really scary."

Katie nodded thoughtfully. That was true.

"Plus there's three of us and one of him," Annabel added, with an evil grin. "We're going too far with this, you know. I mean, nothing might happen – it's just a card, and we're not *certain* it's from him."

"Suppose so," agreed Katie, and Becky nodded.

"We should try asking Mum – you never know, she might just tell us who the card was from. It could be from anybody!" she said hopefully.

"And talking of cards." Annabel got up to grab the pile on the table. "We've got to work out who all these are from!"

Chapter Ten

Katie wasn't worried by the fact that she'd got two Valentine's cards. One was from Robin, obviously – she recognized the writing. The other one had strange Egyptian stamps on and was from Dad – he always sent cards to the triplets as he said they were his favourite girls. Katie reckoned he liked to have any excuse to send them something! He'd put some spending money in too, and Katie decided she definitely wanted to use it to buy stuff for the party that night. Becky's three cards were from Dad, David – and David. He'd tried to disguise his handwriting on the second one, but it was obviously him! Becky tried not to make too much of it, even though she was delighted –

the other two weren't really in the mood, and neither was she when she remembered the card in the silver envelope. They'd tried asking Mum who it was from, but she'd just smiled and said that Valentine's cards were secret.

Annabel had been hoping to do something with Josh that day, although he'd never actually done more than say vaguely that they ought to meet up, so she was free to go shopping. Becky had promised to meet David, but she called him and arranged to get together a bit later so the triplets could all three go into town together. So much had happened over the last few days, and Becky and Annabel had suddenly realized that they'd been neglecting Katie, and each other. They needed some sister-time.

The triplets squashed on to one seat on the bus, giggling, and Annabel started to plan where they were going.

"Can we pop into GirlStuff? Saima said they had some brilliant new hair slides and things when she went in last weekend."

This was very much a question that expected a yes answer – Annabel didn't even wait for it, she just started to rootle through her purse (with difficulty, as she had no elbow room whatsoever) to see how much she could afford to spend on hair slides. Her spending money from Dad had already gone to pay back a loan from Mum for the last time she'd been shopping. "Saima reckoned the nicest ones were about three pounds. Becky, can I borrow—"

"Nope," said Katie firmly.

"I was asking Becky!"

"And I was saying that there's no point asking Becky, 'cause no, you can't go to GirlStuff. We've got serious shopping to do, there's no time for you dithering about over hair clips."

Annabel sighed dramatically. "So where are we going then?"

"That new party shop in the high street, the really cool-looking one."

Annabel brightened up. The shop *did* look

cool, and she'd been wanting to go in for ages. "Excellent. Do you know what you're going to get?"

"No – I'm not sure, just some stuff to decorate the living room. I want it to look really special, but *nothing* to do with Valentine's Day. That's as far as I've got."

Annabel looked thoughtful. She loved parties, and decorating was one of the best bits. "Difficult one."

"What are we going to do tonight, Katie?" Becky asked.

Katie gave her a mysterious look. "Just you wait and see. Megan and I have plans," she said smugly.

The other two tried begging, but Katie wouldn't be drawn. The only thing she would tell them was that Mum was going to let them order pizza for everyone for dinner.

"Cool." Annabel licked her lips. "I'm starving already, breakfast got a bit sidetracked."

Katie made a face. "I still don't want to believe it. But I can't think of anyone else who'd send Mum a card. I wish she'd tell us."

Becky shrugged. "Maybe she's not sure what's going on either."

"You could be right." Annabel nodded seriously. "I mean, if Mum was actually going to go out on a date we'd have to know, wouldn't we?"

They bounced off the bus and headed for Celebration, the new party shop. Katie sighed at the window display, which was very pink and covered in hearts, but Annabel dragged her inside.

"Wow," Annabel breathed, gazing round. The shop had been very cleverly designed to have lots of little nooks and crannies that could be decorated with a theme – she was looking at an indoor fountain, with a life-size mermaid trailing her fingers in the water.

"We don't want a mermaid, Bel," said Katie, grinning. "And we certainly couldn't afford it if we did," she added, grimacing at the discreet little card next to the mermaid model. She was a bit worried that they might not be able to afford *anything* in here.

"Oooh, Katie, come over here!" Becky had wandered over to the far side of the shop.

Katie towed Annabel with her, and found Becky inspecting a display of candles. "Look!" Becky read the sign above the display. "Opening offer – all candles half-price! And they've got some gorgeous ones." She picked up a candle shaped like a flower. "It smells of roses too!"

Katie looked thoughtful. Candles? She hadn't considered that. But yes, they'd fit into her plan very well. Not too girly – provided she didn't go for the pink, rose-shaped ones, anyway – but very cool and party-ish. She hugged Becky. "Well spotted! These are fab." Katie invested in lots of little black and silver floating candles – Mum had a really nice big glass bowl that they'd look great in. Becky bought a couple of the rose-shaped candles as well, for their bedroom, and lent Annabel the money to buy a big purple pillar candle studded with sparkly glass jewels, as she'd clearly fallen in love with it.

Saima, Fran and Megan were arriving at six, but Katie was ready long before that. She'd banished Becky and Annabel and tidied up the living room, borrowing cushions from everywhere in the house to arrange in big comfy piles, finding her favourite CDs, and putting Mum's glass bowl on the coffee table filled with the gorgeous candles. She'd light them just before the others came in so they got the full effect.

She looked round, pleased, but not quite satisfied. She hadn't got a really exciting plan for what they were going to do tonight, except eat pizza and watch videos, and she felt the party definitely needed something more — something that really made it an anti-

Valentine's party, rather than just any old sleepover. She sat down on the sofa to think, and felt something scrunch under one of the cushions. She ferreted around and dragged out a piece of paper with a drawing on – obviously something that Bel had abandoned. Katie peered at the face on the paper – ugh, Josh! She screwed it up and flung it expertly at the bin. As the ball of paper plopped satisfyingly in, the idea she'd been looking for came to her, and she dashed off to find some balloons – she knew they had some in a cupboard somewhere – and various useful bits. The others were going to love this!

She shut herself back in the front room for another half an hour, and then she went upstairs and popped in on Mum, who was working on the computer in the loft. She'd promised to stay out of the way for the evening: unless they really needed her she'd be upstairs.

"Got everything organized?" Mum grinned at her.

"Think so. The money for the pizza's on the kitchen counter, isn't it?"

"Mmmm – have fun."

Katie put her arms round Mum's shoulders and gave her a hug, then turned to go – but not before she'd caught sight of the screen. Mum was reading her emails, and there was one from Jeff Cooper.

So that pretty much answered that then.

Katie decided that now definitely wasn't the time to ask Mum for details – she shouldn't have seen the email, even though she hadn't looked on purpose – and she didn't want to spoil the party by knowing icky details about Mum and their worst enemy's dad. That could wait until tomorrow. She was definitely going to tell Becky and Annabel though – she'd had enough of secrets. Anyway, it was nearly six – she dashed off to root out Becky and Bel.

"You have to come down and wait in the kitchen, OK!" she said bossily.

"OK, OK!" Annabel did her best to sound

huffy, but it was difficult. An evening with their best mates, plus pizza and general lounging about, sounded really cool, and she found that she didn't even mind that she wasn't on a romantic date – much.

She and Becky reported to the kitchen as instructed to be met by a gorgeous smell, the kind of chocolatey smell that they could almost see wafting its way out of the kitchen door and round the hall.

"Wow! What are you making?" Becky sniffed rapturously.

"I invented it. I'm calling it Really Chocolatey Hot Chocolate, and you're going to need it." Katie carefully poured out three mugs of the gloopy brown stuff, and dolloped on marshmallows. When Annabel and Becky were suitably armed against what she was about to tell them – they were *mmm*-ing happily – she took a deep mouthful herself, let it warm her all the way down, and then broke the news. "OK. Mum's got an email from Max's dad, so I reckon it must have been him that sent the card."

Annabel nearly dropped her mug of chocolate. "No! Are you sure?"

"Well, I couldn't exactly ask to read it, could I? But there was definitely one from him. Looks like we're just going to have to face it. But we're not going to let it spoil tonight, OK?"

The other two nodded firmly, and buried their faces in their mugs again. That was the kind of news they really *needed* chocolate for. . .

The triplets were still sitting round the table sipping chocolate when the doorbell rang. Saima, Megan and Fran had managed to coincide on the doorstep, and Katie got them to pile up their rucksacks and sleeping bags in the hall. "And hurry up, OK, because there's chocolate!"

The smell had wafted out to the hall, and Saima, Fran and Megan took no time at all to appear in the kitchen looking starved. Katie grabbed three more mugs. "Can you lot serve up the chocolate – don't forget to give me some – I've just got to go and do the finishing touches in the living room."

She nipped in to light the candles, and then yelled, "Right, you can come in now!" She stood back proudly as they trooped in – she'd turned the lights off, and the big bowl of candles was filling the room with a soft glow.

"It looks great, Katie!" Annabel sounded slightly surprised – she wasn't used to Katie doing this kind of thing.

"It does, doesn't it? Anyway, grab a cushion, all of you, and get comfy." Katie whisked some big bowls of tortilla chips and toffee popcorn from where they'd been hidden behind the sofa, then turned on the DVD player.

"Cool!" Saima squeaked. "What are we watching?"

Katie grinned. "This is *my* party, so we're watching *my* favourite film – *Bend It Like Beckham.* Megan lent it to me."

Megan grinned, but then noticed that the other four were looking slightly less enthusiastic. "Honestly, it's a fab film – you don't have to know much about football, and it's really funny."

Katie settled back on the sofa, budging Megan and Becky over so she could squash in between, and pressed play on the remote. The opening sequence of the film started, and she sighed happily, and grabbed a big handful of popcorn from the bowl on Megan's lap.

"That was excellent!" Annabel said, sounding quite surprised at herself, as she grabbed the remote to eject the DVD two hours later.

"Told you!" Katie stretched, and heaved herself off the sofa. "Hey, we need to order pizza. I'll grab the menu – and then I've got a game while we're waiting." She grinned to herself as she nipped into the kitchen for the menu – she was looking forward to this.

It took a good ten minutes to work out what

to order – and Megan was practically exiled for wanting anchovies. They ended up compromising on pineapple – as Katie said, "At least you can see pineapple if you want to pick it off. I wouldn't even know what an anchovy looked like!"

Once they'd phoned the order through, Katie quickly moved the coffee table, and the various cushions and bowls of snacks out of the way. Then she nipped out to the hall cupboard, where she'd stashed her creation from earlier, and carried it in.

The others stared as she struggled in with it – it was massive.

"What *is* that?" Becky asked, coming to help as Katie tried to turn it the right way round. Suddenly the others started to giggle. Katie had made a huge figure out of balloons, covered it in some old clothes, and taped a paper face on to it. The face wasn't particularly recognizable, but the hair gave it away. It might only be yellow tissue paper, but somehow Katie had managed to give the balloon boy exactly Josh's floppy blond hairdo.

"I thought you might enjoy this, Bel – it's therapy! We're going to squish Josh." Katie stretched the figure out on the carpet. "OK – count of three, we all jump on him. Ready? One – two – three!"

Stamping, jumping and laughing, the six of them burst all the balloons – and Katie had used two whole packets. Eventually they sank back on to the sofa in a giggling pile, and Katie nudged Bel – "Feel better?"

"Definitely!" Annabel sighed happily. "This is great! Loads more fun than yesterday."

"Yeah!" the others agreed, still breathless, and Megan summed it up – "Katie, you're a star. This was the best idea ever!"

Katie smiled. Valentine's Day had turned out to be excellent fun after all!

Read the opening of the
next Triplets book:

Becky's
Dress
Disaster

Becky gazed at her reflection in the mirror and smiled delightedly. She'd never worn anything like this dress before – it was beautiful. She bounced on her toes slightly, and watched the layers of silky skirts ruffle and flounce. It was fab!

"Ftand ftill a minute, dear," muttered the dressmaker through a mouthful of pins. "Jutht need to get the hem level." She crawled round Becky on her knees, adding a pin here and there.

It was the final fitting for the dresses that the triplets were to wear as bridesmaids at their Auntie Jan's wedding in three weeks' time. Becky was really excited – none of the triplets had been bridesmaids before, and she and Annabel had been talking about it for ages.

Carefully making sure she didn't move a muscle from the neck down, Becky glanced over at Annabel – her dress had been adjusted first, and now she was peacocking in front of the mirrors that surrounded the workroom, clearly even more entranced than Becky was. Annabel had played Cinderella in the school pantomime last term, and had a beautiful costume, but this dress was even better.

Auntie Jan was a journalist for a smart homes magazine, and she was *very* stylish. Her wedding was being perfectly designed down to the very last rose petal, and everything was colour-coordinated. Auntie Jan's dress was going to be made of silver-grey raw silk and she was going to have flowers in shades of purple and mauve, and an amethyst tiara. So the triplets' dresses had silvery-white bodices with lilac-coloured skirts to match.

Becky looked at her reflection again, almost shyly – it seemed hard to believe that the princess-like figure in the mirror was her! The silvery-white fabric of the dress brought out the deep blue of her eyes, and made her long golden-blonde hair all sparkly. Next to her Annabel seemed to be thinking the same thing. As the dressmaker heaved herself up off her knees with a sigh, Annabel tiptoed over, moving super-carefully in the precious dress. She stood close to Becky and they gazed at the effect of the gorgeous, identical dresses.

"We look fantastic," said Annabel smugly. She'd never had a problem with false modesty.

Becky grinned at her – she'd never have said it herself, but yes, they did! She looked over her shoulder for Katie, wanting her to share in the excitement. Her other triplet was standing in the corner, waiting for the dressmaker to make the alterations to her dress, and she looked about as unexcited as Becky had ever seen her. In fact, she looked downright sulky. She'd kept her trainers on, and she was irritably scraping the toe of one back and forth on the carpet, and not even looking at herself in the mirror!

"Katie!" Annabel hissed. "Come over here! I want to see all of us together!"

Katie looked round, and shrugged, and just

then the dressmaker, who'd been consulting with Mum about something, bustled back over with her pins and shooed Katie towards the centre of the room.

"This is really so exciting," she continued, still talking to Mum. "I've made dresses for twins before, but never triplets, and they're so completely identical! No one will be able to tell them apart in these frocks."

Mum smiled, but cast a slightly worried glance over at the triplets. They generally weren't keen on dressing alike – she'd had tantrums from them before about wearing matching outfits that their Gran had sent them.

Katie stomped grimly into the middle and stood there, looking as unlike a bridesmaid as it was possible to do in a sticky-out net-skirted dress. She looked like she was going to bite the next person who mentioned the word wedding.

Becky sighed. Katie just wasn't a dress

person – and as for crystal jewellery, and posies, and high-heeled lilac satin slippers. . . She moaned every time they had to go to a dress fitting, and whenever Auntie Jan rang up with more wedding ideas she rolled her eyes horribly, but Becky hadn't quite realized how much she *meant* it. Looking at her now, Becky was starting to feel a teensy bit worried. Katie wasn't going to scowl like that all the way through the wedding, was she. . .?

Annabel didn't seem to have noticed the danger signs. "Katie! You've still got your trainers on, you muppet! You need to put the proper shoes on, or the dress won't hang right!" She clicked her tongue exasperatedly, and exchanged an "honestly!" look with the dressmaker.

Katie sullenly went back to get the high-heeled shoes that the dressmaker had lent them to try on with the dresses, and Becky nudged Annabel. "Do you think she's OK?"

Annabel gave her a blank look. Most of her

brain was filled with sparkly net just now.

Becky went on trying to explain, although she had a suspicion that Annabel wasn't actually capable of processing the idea that someone could not like this dress. "She looks – cross."

Annabel gave Katie a vague glance. "No, she's OK. She's just bored standing around, that's all. Look, Becky, do you think that this dress needs something – I don't know, more twinkly about it? I wish Auntie Jan had gone for that bead decoration I pointed out to her in last month's *Brides* magazine. It would have just added that extra *something*." Annabel pirouetted in front of the mirror, scowling thoughtfully. Perhaps she could . . . no, that wouldn't be fair . . . but then again . . . the other two wouldn't mind, would they? Deep in her daydreams of crystal beads, she entirely failed to register Katie's miserable face, and the concern in Becky's eyes.

Mum didn't seem to have spotted Katie's

bad mood either – she was inspecting the prices of shoes and tiaras and things, and looking slightly worried.

It was definitely up to Becky to do something. She left Annabel trying to work out from which side she looked nicest, and went over to Katie, carefully gathering up the skirt of her dress – it wasn't finally sewn yet, and it was delicate. She edged around the dressmaker, who was measuring Katie's hemline, and stood next to her sister, mulling over the best way to cheer her up. Of course – Katie had been at football practice that morning, and she'd been trying to explain Mrs Ross's new team strategy to them all in the car on the way into town earlier, but Becky hadn't really understood it. Well, she hadn't exactly been concentrating – she tended to zone out when Katie went into football-speak. Now she decided to sacrifice herself. "Katie?"

"Mmm?" It was partly a growl.

"You know that football thing you were

telling us about earlier? The thing Mrs Ross is doing?"

"Mmm?" Slightly less growly, but a bit suspicious-sounding.

"Well, can you tell me about it again, 'cause I didn't get it."

Katie brightened up, and automatically unslumped herself.

"That'th lovely, dear, jutht like that," murmured the dressmaker, who'd been trying to get her to stand up straight for ages.

Katie twitched irritably, but ignored the impulse to kick the stupid dress out of her way. Eagerly she beckoned her sister closer, and Becky gave a secret sigh of relief. Katie had taken the bait. Now, if she could just keep her amused for the rest of the fitting, Katie might forget how bored she was with the whole process. Becky screwed up her face in concentration and prepared to get her head round the complicated explanation that Katie was clearly about to launch into.

"OK, so which bit didn't you understand?" Katie asked enthusiastically.

"All of it," said Becky firmly. She might as well do it properly – in for a penny, in for a pound, as Mum sometimes said.

"Well, Mrs Ross reckons we need to learn to be more versatile. She reckons that if we understand how every player in the team works, then we'll know what to expect from them, right?"

"Ye-es," agreed Becky cautiously. This sounded like sense as far as she could see – Katie hadn't gone into football gobbledegook yet.

"OK, so obviously a striker plays really differently to a defender, yes? And a goalie is just like another kind of thing altogether, so it's really difficult adjusting to the different style of play, but it's going to be completely excellent because. . ." Becky drifted slightly here. She'd caught sight of herself in The Dress (it definitely had capital letters) in the mirror, and she was imagining what her boyfriend, David, would think if he could see her. She smiled happily to herself. There were bound to be loads of photos taken at the wedding. Maybe she could give one of them to David? She had a picture of him that had been taken by chance at the triplets' birthday party last term, but she didn't think he had a photo of her except for silly ones on his phone. She imagined him putting it in a frame and keeping it in his room, and it gave her a little glow inside. Then she jumped – Katie had stopped and was giving her an enquiring look. Becky shot a panicky glance from side to side, but there was no one to help her out, so she plumped for a fifty-fifty chance.

"Oh yes! Definitely!" she exclaimed, nodding furiously, and gazing hopefully at Katie.

Katie looked a bit surprised. She'd just asked Becky if she wanted to meet up with her and Megan in the park the next day so she could demonstrate what she'd been talking about, and she *really* hadn't expected such an enthusiastic reaction.

"Cool! I said to Megan that we'd meet up tomorrow afternoon – she's going to show me some of her goalie moves and I'm giving her pointers on passing. You can try and put some shots past me too!"

Becky realized too late what she'd got herself into and thought fast. "Is it OK if Fran comes too? I said I'd go for a long walk with her and Feathers tomorrow." Actually this had only been a vague suggestion rather than a plan, but Becky reckoned having Fran and Feathers around for the football training session might make it a lot more fun.

"Course!" Katie sounded so happy that Becky felt a little bit guilty. But at least she'd got her sister out of the glooms, that was the important thing.

And with perfect timing, the dressmaker slid the last pin into the hem of Katie's dress. "Done. You look lovely, dear."

Katie just sniffed, and raced – as much as she could in a floor-length dress – to get changed.

Mum spotted her and realized that the fitting was finished. "Oh good – can you two go and get changed as well? Then we can have a look at all the other bits you need."

Annabel had looked mutinous at the idea of taking the gorgeous creation off, but when Mrs Ryan mentioned accessories she moved nearly as fast as Katie had, and it wasn't long before all three triplets were back in their own clothes and gathering round their mother.

Becky grinned to herself as she saw Katie. Now that her sister was wearing her own jeans, trainers and purple hooded fleecy top, she looked like she could breathe again. Of course the dress hadn't actually been made with a corset, but it just seemed to have that effect on Katie. It *was* nice to be able to move without panicking that you were going to tread on the dress, or tear it, or do something else awful, though. Becky felt a bit more relaxed now that she was back in her own green cords and favourite cat T-shirt. Annabel was the only one of the three of them who looked as though she'd felt more comfortable in the dress than she did in her own denim skirt, stripy tights and silver Kickers, Becky mused. Although Bel loved those boots so much that Becky was surprised she wasn't arguing to wear them to the wedding – after all, they'd fit in with Auntie Jan's silver and lilac theme. . .

But now, Bel was looking blissed out by the selection of shoes that was currently being waved under her nose. Mum usually wasn't that keen on the triplets wearing high-heeled shoes, but the wedding seemed to have put that out of her mind. Apparently, heels were a necessity for bridesmaids, although Katie did try and argue for the pretty and, more importantly, *flat* ballet pumps. Annabel was disgusted.

"Katie! Those are for *three year olds*! Are you mad?"

"No!" Katie snapped back. "I just don't fancy breaking my neck in *those*!" She glared crossly at the strappy, silver, high-heeled sandals that Annabel was ogling. "And have you forgotten that this wedding is in the middle of April? Those are going to be really fun if it pours with rain."

"It won't," said Annabel with supreme confidence.

"How do you know?" Katie asked, slightly disconcerted by Annabel's certainty.

"*Because*. It just won't."

Katie smirked, and Mum decided it was definitely time to intervene. "I do think those are a bit too summery, Bel. But these ones are nice, don't you think?" She held up a pair they'd seen already, that actually looked a bit like the ballet shoes, only with small heels. "They're very like the ones you wanted, Katie,"

Mum continued, in a peacemaking tone of voice. "Becky? What do you think? Do you like them?"

"Yes, they're sweet." Becky was uncomfortably aware that she might just have got on the wrong side of both sisters at once – the shoes were pretty, but they weren't nearly glamorous enough for Bel, and they were far too fancy for Katie. As Mum and the dressmaker decided that those were definitely the right ones, Becky sighed. Annabel and Katie were still muttering insults at each other. ("You're crazy!" "Well, you look like you bought all your clothes at a jumble sale – a really bad jumble sale!") She had a feeling that this wasn't going to be the only time between now and the wedding that she would be playing piggy in the middle. . .

Look out for more

Triplets

HOLLY has always loved animals.
As a child, she had two dogs, a cat, and at
one point, nine gerbils (an accident).
Holly's other love is books. Holly now lives
in Reading with her husband, three sons
and a very spoilt cat.

TEN QUICK QUESTIONS FOR HOLLY WEBB

1. Kittens or puppies? Kittens

2. Chocolate or Sweets? Chocolate

3. Salad or chips? Chips

4. Favourite websites? Youtube, Lolcats

5. Text or call? Call

6. Favourite lesson at school? Ancient Greek (you did ask. . .)

7. Worst lesson at school? Physics

8. Favourite colour? Green

9. Favourite film? The Sound of Music

10. City or countryside? Countryside, but with fast trains to the city!